## MORE PRAISE FOR *Trine Erotic:*

"*Trine Erotic* is a beautiful structure of nested narratives. Reading it is like awakening from one dream into another. Evolutionary psychology teaches that narrative was the primal form of speech, and that we learned to speak in order to tell stories. But *Trine Erotic* is not just an engaging story. Alice Andrews makes skillful use of the latest scientific knowledge about the deep evolutionary roots of the modern mind to talk about human nature, women and men, love and sex. The skillful fusion of science with literature is no mean feat, and Andrews succeeds in bringing theoretical concepts to life by embedding them in the lived experience of her characters. I have included *Trine Erotic* on the reading lists for my undergraduate courses on Evolutionary Psychology."

—David Livingstone Smith, PhD; director, New England Institute for Cognitive Science and Evolutionary Psychology; visiting professor, Social and Behavioral Sciences, University of New England; author of *Freud's Philosophy of the Unconscious, Approaching Psychoanalysis: An Introductory Course* and *Psychoanalysis in Question.*

"With this effort, Alice Andrews opens a new genre in fiction: the reflective, biologically informed love story. Primal themes voiced in a very modern idiom. This is not biology in the old sense of simple "animal instincts" or even just the recent sense of selfish genes and the mathematics of human relationship games. It is also biology informed by our modern understanding of how we create and transmit meaning through words. The roles of the "meme" or fuzzy unit of culture, features prominently as a conceptual undercurrent here, but Andrews takes it way beyond being a unit of culture and illustrates by her own masterful example how it is also an agent of human transformation. Through her own storytelling, she seduces the reader into layer after layer of change in their own understanding, all the while explaining what she is doing. This is a relatively novel form of introspective art that both inspires and teaches. Two problems . . . we aren't used to art being quite so aware of its own role, especially in scientific terms, and we usually aren't comfortable with women consciously cutting through the haze of erotic games to see their own relentless Darwinian logic. It's exciting and a bit disconcerting as well to see female sexuality both revealed and unleashed in this light. Alice Andrews could well be one of the most important voices of our times and into the future, and deserves to be very well known."

—Todd I. Stark, author of "Seductive Approaches," "Hypnotic and Subtle Influence," and moderator of Best of Human Behavior and Evolution list/Yahoo

# trine
# erotic

# *trine erotic*

Alice Andrews

ViviSphere Publishing · NEW YORK

This is a work of fiction. Names, characters, places, and incidents are either the products of the author's imagination or are used fictitiously, and any resemblance to actual persons, living or dead, events, or locales is entirely coincidental.

Cover Design by Teal Hutton and Alice Andrews
Author Photo by Rick Lange

Cover image: Cabanel, Alexandre (1824-1889). *Birth of Venus*, 1863. Oil on canvas. Photo: P. Selert.
Copyright © Réunion des Musées Nationaux/Art Resource, NY. Used by permission.

ISBN 1-58776-121-1
Library of Congress catalog number: 2002101071
Printed in the United States of America

**VIVISPHERE PUBLISHING**
A division of NetPub Corporation
2 Neptune Road, Poughkeepsie, NY 12601
www.vivisphere.com    (800) 724-1100

*To every woman's desire
and the art within her.
And for alpha males everywhere.*

# ACKNOWLEDGMENTS

"Do you think this is the only story in you?" a friend asked, after having read "love stories," my seventeen-page short story that inspired *Trine Erotic*. It was a funny question—one which had never occurred to me to ask. I had been compelled to write a story, and so I wrote one. I wasn't thinking about other stories or future stories; wasn't thinking about myself as a "writer."

But it hurt some nonetheless; made me a little defensive: "Of course I have other stories," I told her, as if there were some *value* in that; as if I had some storytelling gene, some story-making module or organ in me which I had to defend; as if to champion this one measly story by proclaiming there were others. But *did* I? I wondered. *Did* I have other stories? And if I didn't, did it matter one way or the other? *Of course not*, I told myself. But as it happened, it wasn't my only story. Who only has one story? (Anyway, it's not just about stories "within." It's also about the compulsion and desire to write them.)

In retrospect, her question was a challenge. But it was also my *shock point*. My waking. To write. Maybe to live. So thank you, Kim, for not being afraid to cause a little pain. There were other friends and family who read that short story whom I'd also like to thank: Jim Andrews, Samantha Bennett, Kay Brover, Lisa Gustin Geiger, Nicole Burman Sichel, and Jessica Wilkinson. A cute dad (who happened to be an artist and writer) on a bench outside a classroom read most of it while we waited for our kids one summer, and I think it was his interest that inspired me to continue.

There were many longer versions that came after that first short story, including the final manuscript. And it was a true pleasure and gift to have friends and colleagues Keith Bardwell, Jacinta Bunell, Victoria Coleman, Rebecca Daniels, Pamela Horn, Monica Grudin, Robert Kelly, Elysabeth Lesnick, Brian K. Mahoney, Nikki Peone, Carla Rozman, Jennifer Ifil-Ryan, Rita Ross, Donal Dionysius Lardner Ward, Beth Elaine Wilson, and Marie Winn read and comment on them. Many, many thanks and sincere appreciation to you all.

I do especially want to thank James Brody, Peter Cooper, Rick Lange, Diane Perlich, David Perry, and most of all, Teal Hutton at Vivisphere, for their critical and in many ways loving attention to the manuscript, from form to content.

And finally, Jason Stern, for his head and heart, for helping add depth to the trinity; for his listening.

Writing is solitary, it's true, but there is always an audience if you dare open yourself, like a book. And that's where the real art comes in. The dialectic. This book is alive. It is constantly changing. Your reading makes it change.

We exist only in the brief instant when we are seduced—by whatever moves us: an object, a face, an idea, a word, a passion.

—*Jean Baudrillard*

Art and nothing but art!
It is the great means of making life possible, the great seduction to life.

—*Nietzsche*

# Conscious Shock

# Third Force

# Conscious Shock

Here Sun and Moon lose their distinction,
In her the triple world is formed.
—Saraha's *Treasury of Songs*

# LOVE STORIES

# soft kill

I want a hot, hot love—so hot,
that when it cools, it almost
burns.

—*Karina Chase*

## *a place for dirty laundry*

I am awake early on a Sunday morning.

My lover and son are asleep.

I drink coffee, read the paper, and every now and then look out my bay windows. It's early, but not still. Things are moving.

A rabbit's hopping near the old, peeling white trellis, scarlet roses everywhere. My tops and panties ripple in the breeze on the clothesline.

And now I see a pretty woman—she must be in her forties—hopping up the stairs to visit my neighbor.

My neighbor is a young, handsome artist, as many men here *are* in this small, artistic town, who earns his rent building houses, as even more men here do. And he's having an affair with a much older, married woman, he once told me, and now, I have just gotten to see her, and I love it. It's voyeuristic, yes, but ultimately soap operaish; because one day, in this town which gets smaller every week, I will meet her, at a parent meeting or at the local farm stand. And I will feel close to her in a way she can't possibly know. She'll probably never know I watched her bound up the stairs to her young lover or that I was reliving that euphoria I had enjoyed many years ago when I first moved here from the city. That we share something.

My then-husband and I had just gotten here when I met a younger man and had an affair. And I know with a certainty that is as fierce as knowing when you love, that it would never have happened back in the city. Not that affairs don't happen there. But there's a fluidity in a small town you don't have in the large city, where things seem more fixed: socially, architecturally, economically—even temporally—who has the time? There's more time where I live now. Here, where there *are* no nannies, jobs are secondary to families, art, and love, even immoral love. Or perhaps especially immoral love.

As a teenager, in the city, I watched a lot of soap operas. I longed to have people show up at my door unexpectedly the way they did on those shows, but it rarely happened. You don't just get on a subway and show up at someone's apartment. What if they're not home? No one has time for that. And then there was the fear of a mugger at one's intercom. So we called and made plans first.

But New Yorkers will also walk by a friend's building without giving a thought about popping in, or up, because apartment buildings are not sexy. Doormen and buzzers, video cameras, intercoms, doors, more doors: there's no seduction. You can't see anything until you're in. If you get in.

The relationship between interior and exterior is more fluid here in the country, where private and public blur. I'm inside, I'm outside, in a matter of seconds. I see plenty that is going on around me. And I can be seen. Here, you really might just "happen to be in the neighborhood," and find me outside gardening or writing or you might even see me in my living room. Houses are approachable. They show skin. They're looser, available, closer to nature. They're penetrate-able. Here in the country, people are unexpectedly in and out of my house all day: friends, neighbors, workers, my kid's friends. The affair, in fact, began with an unexpected visit—the bored housewife's fantasy par excellence.

Showing up out of the blue is romantic. It's tied to the stars, with a sense of fate, not earthbound obsessional scheduling. It's both less committed and more committed at the same time. No calls or plans. But it's real. Fleshy. Immediate. I like the sexy casualness of it; I want to be overwhelmed, to lose control, to submit.

I'm still wondering if all that Clinton/Lewinsky coverage I was exposed to before I moved here had something to do with my lapse of moral character, and my confessional mode. "Clinton's Europeanized us," I told my then-husband, "he's made the American affair almost de rigueur."

It was a powerful meme, this cheating meme. (The word *meme* was coined by Richard Dawkins in 1976. A meme is the cultural equivalent of a gene—an element of a culture that is passed on by non-genetic means, especially by imitation, like: ideas, tunes, fashions, and customs. A group of memes, like those found in a religion, a book—even an essay—are called memeplexes, at least for now. Though I wish they'd come up with another word, like *memesome*. It sounds better and it makes sense—a chromosome is to genes, what a memesome is to memes.)

Anyway, I heard the unfaithful meme loud and clear, from just about everywhere: *Adultery is okay. In fact, it's pretty good, and everyone does it. Ha, ha. We're human.* If you think the percentage of affairs didn't go up after our great model, our father figure, Clinton, was exposed, you don't understand memes. It's like our dad gave us permission to stay out late. He was like the weed-smoking parent we stole pot from. It's not that I blame my infidelity on Clinton or the memes. I made the decision. But there's no question I was influenced.

It's almost noon. The guys are up and playing in the yard. I see the married woman's car still. And I know what she is doing. I am *that woman*. (Aren't we always?) I'm also that trellis, a little worn, in some ways damaged. And the roses: tangled, revealing, growing. And that pink tank top flapping in the wind on the clothesline, drying in the hot May sun.

It's nice, I think, drinking my now cool coffee, to dry clothes on a clothesline. I certainly don't need to. I have something most city dwellers deeply covet: my very own laundry room. And it's good that I do, too, because here in this soapy, small town, which gets smaller every day, and where the physical space allows you to feel alive, life is pretty messy. But oddly, there is room for it.

*i n a t t e n t i o n*

That's what Sarah read in the local, freebie arts magazine.
And it put her in a mood. A frustrated mood. She felt sort of
envious of its liberated author. And since it was a local paper,
she started to imagine the women it could be. She looked at
the byline. It had to be a pseudonym. *Willa Wiley?*

*Erich.*

*Erich.*

She gazed out the screen of her porch and watched a house
finch dart from a blooming black locust tree to an oak. She
wondered about that finch.

She wondered why she was thinking of her old college lover, too.

Erich.

How did he manage to find his way from her baby toe (that's where she told herself she kept him) into her heart and head just like that? Just from reading some confession about an affair in her hometown, in her local rag. She forced him back into her toe. He had no business moving around her body like that.

She was in the kitchen stirring Bolognese sauce when she heard Jonathan come down the stairs. He had been asleep in the kids' bedroom. Sarah hated this, of course, when he fell asleep in the afternoon or early evening. It threw the family's understood rhythm off. Dad wasn't around to talk to. And further, it meant sometimes he'd wake up when she was just setting off to bed and then be up stirring around their room at two in the morning. It was a weak way to control things, she often told him, and he honestly didn't understand what she meant. And it was a little odd and revealing, too. Why not sleep in his own bed?

He walked into the den where the kids were playing, gave a kiss on the head to Maggie and a pat on the shoulder to Nicholas, and went out to the screened porch where Sarah had retired to again. Erich was safely in her toe by this time, and she was onto thinking about her town in a way she hadn't before—and her house as sexy—memes she'd pass on to her friends, in one way or another.

Jonathan picked up the same artsy magazine Sarah had read "A Place for Dirty Laundry" in and began flipping through the pages, sneezing.

"Bless you," she said, "allergies bothering you?"

"Yeah. When aren't they?"

"I'm sorry . . . You know, you might want to try that homeopathic remedy I told you about."

"Maybe I will . . . this antihistamine makes me feel terrible and I'm still sneezing," he said without once looking at her.

"I've got this baby theory—a really good one—you wanna hear it?" Sarah said.

(Baby theory being her term for her speculations.)

"Uh-huh . . . Okay." He was looking at a photograph of a clothesline with pretty underwear on it.

"It's been on my mind for years and years and I never said anything to you about it. Can you believe? . . ." He continued flipping the pages.

"No, I can't, what is it?" he said, eyes now fixated on an ad about Internet chat rooms.

"Well, it's that allergies are sexually transmitted—that they can be sexually transmitted. . . . What do you think? . . . Jon?"

"What?" he said.

"Allergies . . . I think maybe they're bacterial or something."

"I dunno. Why do you think?"

"Well, it wasn't very long after I started sleeping with you that I got hay fever. And, well, for fun I've been doing a sort of case history thing . . . collecting the allergy and sexual histories of friends here and there and others who didn't mind divulging such intimacies . . . you know me . . . people in Dr. Thoerno's waiting room, on the supermarket line," she said, smiling.

Jonathan continued to flip pages.

"My *n* is small, of course, and not statistically significant, but there *is* something there. There's a correlation. Practically everyone I've talked to who's developed allergies as an adult has done so only *after* sexual contact with someone with allergies. I don't have a control, of course. But what I'm think-ing is that there's a switch. And a person has a particular heri-table predisposition, and certain environmental factors—like overexposure to chemicals, pollution, and, I'm thinking . . . an 'infected' carrier—can turn it on. Without these triggers, someone with a high genetic probability of getting allergies— say seventy percent—which is a person's chance if both their parents have allergies—could avoid them. Or with too many of these triggers, someone *without* a genetic predisposition, could get them. Whatdaya think?"

Jonathan heard the question. But the last thing he wanted to do was have a conversation about this, to engage her. He was irritated by her passion for ideas. He just wanted to look at the magazine, relax, and not think—be in her presence, just not talk. She talked so damn much. He really didn't care about allergies and genetics. But he depended on that mind of hers. And he liked sex with her. A lot. Even after all these years and the kids. Even though *she* seemed to have lost inter-est. And he knew that without *some* response, without the requisite "rapporting," there'd be no sex.

But he had a problem. Disagreeing with her theory only meant one thing: more talk. But agreeing with her theory would amount to admitting he was the cause of her suffer-ing—being partly to blame for her sickness—and her sick-ness, *of course*, had to be genetic.

"I dunno. Could be," he said, looking at her for the first time. And he went into the kitchen for a beer, took a piece of bread, and poured some sauce on it. He thought it was deli-cious and kept it to himself. Later at dinner, he would thank her for the meal, and make sure the children did as well, but that would be it. It was his lesson to her: to not wish for praise.

So, I hope you weren't wanting to hear about how humid it was out there on the porch; every last detail about the wicker chairs they were on. More physicality. More sights, sounds, smells, tastes. Because I can't do it. I won't . . . I don't want to. So, if that's what you're looking for, I want to let you know up front, before we go any further, you're not really going to get that. Not that much. In fact, I'm not sure what you're going to get, or if you'll get anything. I'll give you what I can. And you can take what you need. If it's not enough; if it's not what you want, that's okay. That's the nice thing about a book. You can leave it and it won't feel bad. Though how many books have you started and were unable to finish, only to feel badly anyway? But there's no reason to feel bad. When you can't finish a book, it's usually because it doesn't give you pleasure in some way. It's not *your* fault. It's just the wrong fit. Of course, a book can't give you pleasure every moment. You must work at helping it give you pleasure sometimes . . . must be artistic and patient.

You think I'm trying to manipulate you, don't you? No. I'm not trying to do that. There's a lot I'm trying to do here, but get you to read this book—love this book—that's not it. Okay, I'll try to refrain from interjecting. It's very distracting. I'm sorry.

Though Jonathan had never been all that interested in Sarah's baby theories, at least before, in the beginning years, about fifteen now, he had tried to pay attention. So, when she first noticed his inattention a few years ago, she tried everything:

"Jon. Come on! Look at me with those bottle-green eyes when I'm talking," and she'd hold his face tenderly, maternally, and then squeeze his cheeks until his lips pursed. They'd laugh and joke about it. And it worked for a while—until it just wasn't funny anymore; until it was serious; until it didn't work.

It wasn't a secret that this was one of the few places Jonathan had any control with her. She had to be content with his shallow ear. Discontent meant an argument—about getting him to listen to her—and this always got her nowhere; got her talking about his attention and not, say, her idea about the evolutionary reason for grief. So she was content, for a while, with their setup. At least this way, she got to *tell* her baby theories—even if it was to a man who didn't want to listen; to a man whose eyes were focused on a photograph of pretty panties; to a man who'd never bother to read the essay that went with it. Somehow, just the communication of these ideas was enough, as if the ideas guided *her*, not the other way around. As if the memes themselves kept her from arguing so they could just be freed into the ether.

After dinner, after the kids were asleep, Sarah was putting away dishes and Jon came into the kitchen.

"Can I tell you about my dream?" he said.

"Sure, of course," she said.

And she sat down with him at the farm table in the middle of the kitchen.

"Okay, I'm at a river. And there's all these trees flanking it. Bending over it. And I'm in a boat. And the trees are black locusts. And they're in bloom. And it's white everywhere. Blossoms everywhere. And I realize this and take a deep breath in to smell them—and I smell nothing. And I cry. And the blossoms start raining down on me and I'm covered in them and . . . and I'm suffocating in them."

"Oh, that's not too good. What do you think?"

"I don't know. You're the idea woman. Miss psychoanalytic. You know I don't have a head for that stuff."

"Well, of course, there's lots of lenses and models to use to interpret it. But just looking on the—"

"You know what, I don't really want to hear, actually. I'm sorry."

"What is it? Why do you *do* that?"

"Do what? Decide I don't want to hear some Freudian-Jungian analysis of my dreams?"

"Well, yes. Get me all excited about it and then withdraw, retreat . . ."

"I'm sorry . . . what I think I need is . . . to go into therapy—I need to talk to an objective party, about my dream-life, about everything."

"Oh, Jon, that's wonderful. That's really good. . . . I wonder if maybe the dream helped. You know I've been wanting you to go for years!"

"You know what, Sarah? I don't want to hear *that!* Okay? This isn't about *you* and how *right* you are all the time," he said, escalating it five notches out of proportion. "And I'm through talking about this with you! I don't want to hear your voice!"

"Come on, Jon, don't be like this. . . . Everything was nice. It was nice. Why get so upset? I only point out things I've been right about so that maybe you'll listen to me a little sooner next time."

"You know what, Sarah, just leave me alone." And he went upstairs.

And she said, though he wasn't listening, "Fine. I'm going out."

Sarah was glad for an excuse to go into the village. The balminess of the air was seductive, almost musky, and it was always exciting to be in a place without the kids or Jonathan, even if it wasn't far away, as if she were starting over and anything could happen. She went into Wind Over Café and ordered a large decaffeinated latté. She overheard a very large man with a buzz-cut and a napkin tucked into his brown plaid shirt talking to himself in different accents. She had always had particular respect for the mad—it couldn't be a coincidence that throughout history (or maybe just literature) it was the insane who were the prophetic, the Cassandras, the wise fools. She knew in her core that madness, art, and genius were related to truth somehow, and so she listened carefully to the man dribbling soup down his chin; maybe he had something to say about the coming year:

*Two percent reduction, school chancellor fixin' Nixon 'nam bush baby, push baby, look again, they've been laden, plagued . . .*

She couldn't make it out—he was talking too low and the café was abuzz with perhaps less interesting chatter.

After spending an hour or so at the café, Sarah went home. Jon was sleeping. The kids were sleeping. Sarah had a burst of energy. Was it her night out at the café alone which invigorated her? Was she unconsciously relieved Jon was going into therapy? Was it not decaf? Shit! It wasn't decaf! Goddamn it. The woman who was serving her was in the midst of what seemed to *her* great Windhover gossip and dipped her scooper into caffeine grinds. She decided to clean the downstairs closets. Then it was the pantry. Now she was feeling tired and wired. It was four AM. She went to bed because her body was tired but her brain was ecstatic—churning out one beta wave after another. By six AM her throat hurt and by seven she was asleep. Jon woke her up several times, but she told him to let her sleep and he got the kids off to camp. At noon, Sarah awoke to the whine of a nearby lawn mower and realized that she was sick. From the rumple of her bed she began to write furiously, uncontrollably.

She was compelled.

She wrote about how little in common she had with Jonathan despite the similarities of their views. His interest in science was too pragmatic and superficial for her; he didn't probe the difficult philosophical questions which burned in her and made her (just as her children made her) go on. She wrote about how she yearned to go out to a romantic dinner, drink a little wine or a lot and talk passionately all night about the neural and genetic basis of behavior:

> To be turned on by a man who thinks deeply about evolutionary theory, bioethics, the reason for grief, the holographic paradigm, the mind-body problem, the Chomsky-Piaget debate, the Gould/Wilson/Wright debate. A soul mate.

> I was twenty-two and out of college. I was living in a big studio in Red Hook. The guy who had been renting it before me was an adjunct in the film department at Bard. He had shown the place to me twice. I rented it and he moved just down the street. We'd say hello getting into and out of our cars—mine, an old, pale blue Karmann Ghia, his, an old, red Valiant. It was cold that winter and I guess he knew how leaky the windows were in my apartment. (He was now warm in the upstairs of a newly refurbished two-family Queen Anne Victorian.) He asked me if I wanted to borrow his portable heater and came over with it that night. He stayed. We talked for hours—maybe five or six. He said, "I used to imagine a bed just like this [it was an old iron bed I had found with friends in Poughkeepsie] right here [to the side of the fire place] like this [it was against the whitewashed brick wall like a daybed]." It was an unusual place to put a bed, certainly, and somehow his prescient vision made me feel destined to be with him. Or, at the least, with him that night in that bed. We lasted a couple of months. I was warm that whole winter.

Erich once said if we hadn't met at school we would've met somewhere else—New York City, maybe, or Berlin. That was pretty romantic for Erich. With Jon there was never any of that. No feeling of being destined for him. At least, he never said anything and that's usually what did it for me.

With marriage and children comes the inevitability of—

The modern clichés—the memes about marriage she'd absorbed from the popular culture of her youth began flashing in her brain. She was afraid of those memes. The *hot love/ warm love* meme. The *marriage stifles* meme. To write them down would make it *real*. But Erich came to her mind anyway. The unconscious doesn't know *No*.

*Erich.*

She felt a warmth rise from her stomach up into her chest. Or was it from her toe?

*Erich.*

She could hear him. His voice.

"I should like to patent that," he had once told her.

Her mouth was pure desire. Every suck was from the heart and between her legs.

The deeper she took him in was her way of saying *I love you* deeper. He couldn't go far enough for her, although it hurt. Her love for him made her do things she would have told her friends never to do. Her endurance of pain inflicted by him was limitless and she never tired of tests: sexual pain, emotional pain, physical pain other than sexual, like a kick in the gut or a whack in the face. The pain somehow, of course, made the love that more intoxicating. Later she would recall to Jonathan that it was her numbness that craved the pain— at least then she could feel.

Jonathan. He had spent much of his young adult life feeling as if something were missing. But then he went off to graduate school at Yale and met Sarah the first week. She was not only beautiful, she was sensitive, soulful, sensual and big-hipped. And she didn't wear makeup! She fulfilled him. And yes, the fact that she had the kind of mind that couldn't stop synthesizing and generating new ideas repulsed him. But it attracted him, too. It was what he longed to have in himself. But it didn't seem right on her. It was like overdeveloped quadriceps—nice on him, not so nice on her. At least, according to the popular culture.

But Jon needed her ideas. (Like her ideas needed her.) He depended on them over the many years they had been together. He sort of wore them like his beloved Armani suits. Except when Sarah was speculating about Lamarkian traits, allergy qua infection, and other too far-flung-for-Jon scientific ideas, their minds seemed to work together as one smooth, epistemic engine. And this suited them. They churned out their position on political issues, art and culture, people and places. They talked about how we see and hear and how we're conditioned. Sarah had got him on this. Why was it, she wanted to know, when watching old movies, actors seem so stilted? *They don't seem "real." We can see that they're "acting." It's like we're able to see their art more clearly now.* And she'd go on: *Actors today seem so "real"—we aren't able to see their craft. But I bet we will in fifty years.* And she saw the same thing with music: *Today it sounds fine adding dissonant tones to a chord, but it would have sounded just awful to earlier listeners.*

Along the same lines, Jonathan had been pleased to find a real story in an historical book, which he often brought up at dinner parties, about a Spanish oil painter whose art had been forged in the sixteenth century. It was the old Vermeer story.

For hundreds of years, no one—lay people and art experts alike—could see it. Until this century. *And now*, he'd say, as if this were his idea, *anyone can recognize that they are not only forgeries, but sentimental, nostalgic, poor representations of the brilliance of this Spanish painter.*

They both knew these shared positions were, in fact, not shared. They were *her* positions. Jonathan didn't really know what he thought half the time. He was a lost man without her. And so, because he was unsure of himself, he played echo. As a united front with her, he could be rooted. It wasn't an unusual dynamic, certainly. They had friends whose relationships had similar morphologies, except in those couples, it was always the women who were unsure of themselves, parroting the alpha males, living through them. Sarah wanted to feel fine about this modern reversal. But it was hard. Jon made her feel like a shrew. What she needed was a man who was more whatever she was than *she* was. An alpha to tame her. But somehow, she didn't know this, or get it, perhaps never would.

So together, though it was really Sarah, they were politically active in left-of-center politics, though privately, guiltily shared conservative thoughts they didn't dare tell their liberal and socialist friends. And they were smart and morally disciplined enough to be suspicious of their sometimes seemingly conservative beliefs, understanding their fleetingness, the transitoriness of them. They were proud of their decent social actions in the world, and felt little dissonance living with this moral contradiction.

Like when workfare came to the nearby city of Windhover, they rallied against it. *It was too tough on people—it didn't train people for the stinking jobs it gave them—sometimes leading to injury—and it paid them far less than they could have gotten if they had obtained the job without workfare,* they decried. *And then there was the limit. With welfare, if you couldn't find a job, you were supported by the government for as long as necessary. Workfare cut you off—kids or no kids.*

In the real world they knew workfare was bad for the un-employed—but in theory they both agreed it was better. Wel-fare was terrible. It kept people at the basest standard of liv-ing and it didn't empower them. It didn't get them out of the house working—making contacts, friends, feeling good about themselves, having their kids see them go off to work. All the things the Right might have said but not necessarily believed. And sometimes their positions often seemed right-wing to their liberal friends when, in fact, they were libertarian. Like siding with Haydn, Jonathan's brother, a gun manufacturer down south. Sarah and Jonathan always got into hot debates at dinner parties when defending Haydn, defending the right of all citizens to bear arms.

Jon's feelings of inadequacy, whether they stemmed from this or from the tauntings about being scrawny when he was a kid (*he* showed *them*), the maltreatment he received from his large and bullish brother Haydn, the whippings from his fa-ther, were quite unrelated to his present life, however. Jon was a successful and handsome lawyer. He was a logical man and had a strong sense of justice. He generally defended envi-ronmental agencies and organizations and even worked for the Justice Department on occasions. Greenpeace International used his counsel often, as well as Wildlife Now! He even had a recent brush with fame—a short interview on *Nightline* and the *Today Show*—since he was involved in a huge class action suit *against* several environmental agencies including the EPA, and because he was attractive. It was an odd case, involving a community in Washington State which had been hit hard by a ruling that protected the forests but not their livelihood.

Jonathan was likely to win, too (along with his colleagues), as he had so many times before.

No one, not even Jonathan himself, questioned his success. But it was that unsure, beaten young man who more than haunted him, who stirred in him his past feelings of failures real or imagined and threw him off emotional balance. His old sense of himself lingered in the shadows like a ghost. And he couldn't shake it.

## *what pulls*

In some ways, it was finally Jonathan's lack of appreciation and understanding of Sarah and the "will" of her little allergy theory that made Sarah finally move. Outside the home. Beyond Jonathan. It wasn't her usual way. She wasn't a toward-the-world woman. It wasn't her nature. Sure, she was a science writer, and a person has to be driven in some way to get published. But fortunately, she had been able to leave the toward-the-world gestures to agents, colleagues and friends to help her publish. She did the writing—that was it. Her science column, which appeared in the big Albany paper every Wednesday, and which was a cross between Natalie Angier and Diane Ackerman (sexier than Angier, more technical than Ackerman), had been edited and compiled in an attractive book called *Science for Everyone* by a friend. Then there was the even and socially responsible *The Nurturing of Nature: What Schools Can Do to Bring out Children's Highest Potential*, which was mostly a synthesis and review of the latest information coming from the fields of developmental psychology, sociology, and pediatric neuropsychology. But it was her baby theory par excellence that sat in manuscript form, unpublished, on her desk. It was short and provocative, and it was all hers—*Evolutionary Psychology, Epigenesis and the Plasticity of Mind.* But scientific speculations are hard to publish. You have to be a Carl Sagan, an E.O. Wilson. Sarah had a B.S. in environmental science/psychology and an M.F.A. in science writing—she wasn't exactly a great academic.

The natural and obvious turn, then, for Sarah, was toward her computer, which worked its seduction on her, connecting her otherwise toward-the-home writer's life with the rest of the world. Before e-mail, she might not have called John Atterboro, Nobel Prize laureate/scientist, with her baby theory. But that "send" button, the anonymity, the way that it offers a gift of non-commitment to the recipient—it's easy not to return e-mail—harder to get off the phone or not return a call—helped her turn toward the world. And his e-mail address was right there on the back of his book, *Evolution of Infectious Disease*, beckoning her.

The book was unquestionably controversial. Despite Atterboro's high standing in the scientific community, *Evolution of Infectious Disease* was basically rejected by the medical establishment. His theory—and this was no baby theory—was that heart disease, cancer, Alzheimer's, and psychiatric illnesses are caused by various infections. It seemed logical that he might consider allergies within this range of diseases, and so she wrote him about her baby theory and pressed send.

☞

A week went by; it was late at night and the house was asleep. Sarah's eyes were burning, but she was beginning to really enjoy e-mail and the freedom of surfing inanities on the Internet. In her In-box was something from atterbor@amherst.edu. She opened it:

Sarah:

I'm sorry it took so long to get back to you. I've just had back surgery and it has slowed me down. Your allergy case study is intriguing. Your notion of a switch could answer some of my opponents who continue only to see genetics, diet, and stress as contributing to heart disease. As you know, we are now linking heart disease to Chlamydia pneumoniae. But if the bacterium is turning on a switch, rather than directly causing heart disease, it would be of stunning, synthetic importance. We could worry less about "multifactorial" nonsense and work on the genetic switch. Please send your case study for review. I will be in contact.

Cheers,
John

She replied to some friends and family and saved what were probably queries and comments from people interested in her books and articles for later, and then clicked on Northernlight, her favorite search engine. Earlier that month, Sarah had heard about NASA's Magellan Project. The Working Group for Planetary System Nomenclature (a committee of the International Astronomical Union) was assembling the names. The part that interested her was their invitation to the public to name topographical features of Venus. Under NASA's guidelines, the nominated name should be that of a deceased American female citizen, notable or worthy of the honor in some way and have no religious, military, or national significance. Sarah had thought about her mother, Margaret Huyck Fjørtoft. She was all of those things. She had been a doctor who had made important contributions to the field of cardiovascular disease, receiving a Scientific Achievement Award and the Dr. Charles Beaumont Award in Medicine at an early age.

But now, she had the chance to immortalize her mother, pay homage to her, and put her in the heavens. Sure it was just impact craters and volcanic calderas, but this was the closest thing to God, for a materialist. She searched the World Wide Web.

At the "search" icon, she typed:

MAGELLAN PROJECT VENUS NAMES.

She clicked on "search."

3,524,578 matches.

She clicked on the closest sounding site:

www.jpl.nasa.gov/magellan.

There she found the e-mail address she was looking for, along with a "snail mail" address: kaleb@kelvin.jpl.nas.gov. Venus Names Magellan Project; Office Mail Stop; 233-21Jet Propulsion Lab; 4181 Oak Grove Drive; Carmena, California 98721.

She copied this to her desktop and went back to the previous page.

Maybe it was because of that essay she read in the local paper—that meme she was afraid of—that freed her to click NETFIND—e-mail.

Then SEARCH.
U.S. / INTERNATIONAL. She clicked on INTERNATIONAL.
She was feeling like Magellan.
Click.
ERICH SCHWERT. Click.
SEARCHING. . . .
3 matches were found:
ERICH SCHWERT.
erichschwert@yahoo.ge.com
ets@login.eunet.net
nisus@oxford.edu
They were both philosophy majors at Vassar; he had to be "nisus" and at Oxford. And what a rebel . . . he had to have had the only e-mail address at Oxford without his actual name attached to @oxford.edu. Erich . . .

She e-mailed him:

Erich—

Ah, e-mail. Old girlfriends from across the world, across almost decades . . . just like that.

For many reasons you've been on my mind lately. A shadow really.

And a lot of things bring me to this question I want to ask you. A novel I'm thinking of writing. Too much evolutionary psychology. My interest in love.

I still remember the day you and I went to the city to see the Van Gogh exhibit at the Met—it's almost twenty years now. We were sitting on the steps of the museum

thinking about getting on a train back to Poughkeepsie.
You had loved a painting of that yellow chair and so I
got you a post card of it and wrote something inconse-
quential, except, I signed it "Love, Sarah."

I recall not thinking much about that signing, feeling
free about it, because you had actually done it before in
a few notes to me, and I had figured "lots of love" and
"Love, Erich" were basically empty when I received
them—as meaningful as "Dear" is to one's tax attorney.
So you read this post card there on Fifth Avenue, and
said, "Do you?" And I said, "Do I what?" And you said,
"Do you love me?" And you must have seen it. Maybe
even before I did. I did love you and I said so—or maybe
I just said "Yes." And do you know what you said to me?
You said, "I like you, too." A criminal thing, I think.
But perhaps not as much as what came after.

I remember my face got very, very hot—I'm sure quite
red. And my heart, something went wrong there, too.
Then, a few moments later, you laughed and said, of
course, you loved me, too. But now I wonder if you were
telling me the truth. Every time you told me that year
that you did, you must have been lying. Though it has
taken me many years to figure it out. And I don't understand it, but I do.

The question is . . . since you didn't love me in the first
place . . . why did you torture me by asking me if I
loved you? And then why lie and say that you did and
continue to lie even when I tried leaving you several
times? We could have just gone on the way we were, and
I would have kept that feeling to myself, perhaps not

understanding it, not giving it a name. Not giving it power.

So why, Er? Why did you lie?
—Sarah

P.S.
I hope you are well, of course. And, if you do write back . . . please don't point out sentence fragments—you were always critical of my prose. The fragments are intentional. And what are you doing at Oxford?

She didn't expect a reply to her insane e-mail, but it was fun writing and even more fun sending.

It was August now and Nicholas and Maggie were at sleepaway camp. Sarah and Jonathan had always looked forward to Augusts together, though they missed their children more than either thought healthy. Especially Sarah. Separation was difficult for her on account of all the death in her family. That's what that numbness was about. The numbness which asked Erich to give up his pain to her. She lost her sister Sally to an overdose of a very bad mix of heroin, cocaine and speed which was meant to mask the pain of losing their parents in a car crash when they were so young. Perhaps Sarah overcompensated for her need to want to keep her children by her every moment, by allowing them to be freer than most kids seemed to be. She didn't want to over-protect them. It was her way of loving them. By not giving in to her needs to envelop them.

But things were different this August. Jon had begun therapy. He seemed angrier and harder to deal with. And Sarah was finding that what she liked most about him was disappearing in his twice a week therapy sessions. She confronted him about their relationship, as she had done many times before. She talked about separation, though it was hard for her. But he was averse to talking about it. He stonewalled her. He wanted to do what he always did: ignore it until he did enough chores around the house and told enough jokes that she soon forgot. But the kids weren't around and somehow this made it easier to be wed to her idea.

So Jonathan lived in that house, then, like a shadow, trying to be good, trying to listen, trying to do the dishes, trying to understand why, with her life as tough as it had been, she could be so tough. It was simple, really. It was her intense Dionysian nature. Jonathan knew he would never have made it as far as she had, had he had her life. But he also thought this life of hers, this life filled with death, is what gave her the quality he felt lacking. And he felt miserable for envying her. He could never tell her. It's not that he wished *his* parents had been killed in a tragic accident, or that his brother Haydn was dead and gone, of course. He just wanted what came out of it all—her depth and complexity. But, as she would sometimes explain to him, knowing how he envied her: "You have to lose something. And it's not loss that hands depth and complexity to you automatically, but the process of grief—the layers of synaptic protection and defense, a restructuring of ego and identity. The words (the signs) 'depth' and 'complexity,' a metaphor for what really happens (signified) morphologically, physically, in the brain."

Another baby theory—this one, postmodern and neurological. Every time Sarah used those terms "sign" and "signified," Jon felt queasy. She had explained those terms to him before, but he always forgot, and that in itself made him feel bad.

⌒

Sarah's grief was made harder by the fact that she and Sally were the daughters of scientists, brought up as atheists. There was no heaven to console them; the girls knew where their parents were—they weren't. Their ashes had been strewn into the pond in the back of their grandparents' house. Sarah even played with the idea of becoming a Mahayana Buddhist later in college, to make up for the pain of having had nothing to rely on in the face of too much death, but she was too much of a material girl for it to last longer than a semester.

And just as Sarah was developing a real relationship with her grandmother, the woman had a stroke and was completely paralyzed. Sarah took care of her that whole last year in high school.

Everyone prayed Vassar would save her. Her Norwegian grandmother, Tsoka, was especially saddened Sarah's beauty had been wasted on grief and nursing. Tsoka told her on the phone, *I want you to be happy. I want you to find a nice boy. I want you to do this for your Momo, will you? You do it for me?*

Tsoka thought Sarah was afraid of truly living, afraid of men. And the *Mormor* was right. Sarah wasn't sure she believed that it was better to have loved and lost than to have never loved at all. She lived in fear that something bad would happen and she held her breath most of the time, waiting.

At Vassar is where she met Erich. It was orientation week. There was a party at a dorm and her roommates dragged her. Men herded around her, of course, but not one was able to penetrate her deep, sad intensity. They were all so young and dopey, how could they? Then a guy tried to lure her to his room with a story about a flag he had on his wall (and really about his blueish blood), which had belonged to his great-great uncle or something, and how it hung at the White House while the great-great-grandfather had been secretary of state. She didn't really care. She was being nice showing the little interest she did. When they got to the room however, there was an intriguing older guy there in a black leather jacket. He seemed sleepy.

"Hullo," he said, in some kind of European accent.

"Hi, I'm Sarah," she said watching his head fall down for a moment and come back up again.

"Pardon my nodding off . . . I'm a narcoleptic."

"Oh," she said. And she was hooked.

She actually believed him, too.

Erich.

Count Erich Schwert. (The titles were from his British mother's side.) He liked to call himself Master Erich and sometimes Lord Schwert. He was impossible about it. And he demanded, sardonically, that others should call him that as well. "That's Lord Erich . . . to you," he'd say. And they all fawned and let him get away with it, too.

Sarah wasn't impressed by his titles. Not really. Though sometimes, she'd catch herself humming, "It Was So Romantic"—the song Cinderella sings in the old Disney classic. So the Count crap must have struck a fairy tale chord, somewhere in her. (Countess Sarah . . . Lady Sarah . . . )

Erich was twenty-one, which is old for a freshman. In fact, he missed the cut-off by two years, but they made an exception for *him*. And on top of that, he was there for free: tuition, books, room—he even managed to get them to pay for his Marlboro's. Why all the fuss for some late-bloomer? It wasn't because he was titled. It was on account of his father, a German expressionist painter who had been a visiting professor at Vassar back in the '30s and '40s.

The painter, who had had Erich in his sixties, and who was at the time living in Arles, had a certain mystique about him—the fact that he had fathered eight children, six from different women, certainly helped. But perhaps it was a certain well-known quote that traveled the campus like a brush fire and burned its way onto the cool undergraduates' psyches, which left a hot, glowing aura around anything Schwert: "There is only one good purpose of a woman's mouth, and it damn well isn't to talk."

So it went. Funny Sarah hadn't heard it. Anyway, the point is, the old painter's mythology just added exponentially to Erich's own seductive mystique. His sexual charisma was, after all, his birthright, his legacy. It was all quite natural to him: his roving eye, jealous nature, good looks—his stinging wit. He was not only born—he was bred an alpha. Even if the womanizing tendency hadn't been innate, what young man could grow up hearing about his father's exploits and prowess (rumors he dated this actress and that, only marrying one of the mothers of his children) and not attempt to compete, to live up to the unspoken expectations?

And Erich was clearly something different. That's what appealed to Sarah. She thought maybe he had known death, too. He certainly had a dark side. He was very tough. Too tough, actually. He used to hit her. And for the worst reasons, too. One time he hit her because she asked him to hold her while they were sleeping in that very small bed. So what, he was tired? Was that any reason to pummel her? Oh, and he was a terrible drug addict. Any drug seemed to do, though narcotics, any opiate-derived substance, was much preferred. She didn't even know about it until she already loved him. She loved him so much. It was her first time loving. She would never be able to love like that again.

And what's crazy about this is that, at least in the beginning, she started hanging out with him for her Mormor. He was interesting to her, when she first met him, but that was it. But she wanted to be able to tell Tsoka she was with some-one. And so because she didn't want to lie, she hung out with Erich at first, so that Tsoka could stop worrying.

If she had known what she was getting into, how deep her love would be, how painful it would be in the end . . . ah, but perhaps that was its strength. Not knowing. Not know-ing about love.

There were many times she tried to leave him, especially after he hit her, but he would beg her to stay. He'd say, "I have no friends, don't leave me," and "Please don't leave me, I *lovf* you." And she loved him. His words pulled her. Physically. Not morally. She couldn't leave. After he left her for the Brazil-ian actress exchange-student who lived off campus, she was so bad, she ended up in emergency at Ulster County Hospital. She believed air was leaking out of her chest and was so convinced—and convincing—she had college security drive ninety miles an hour to get her there. When she arrived, things only got worse; they thought she was on drugs. How they came to this conclu-sion is unclear, because her eyes were as clear as spring water—no dilation, no bloodshot, nothing. Yet she was hysterical. They were able to establish fairly quickly there weren't any holes in her chest. The attending physician lacked imagination to see that Sarah was probably having a psychotic episode—what a kind therapist would later call *creative, artistic.*

In all fairness to the doctor, there were quite a few kids com-ing in on bad trips and with other drug-related problems from the schools in the area, so it was a reasonable assumption. But the staff was relentless in their questions about her "supplier." She never understood why a hospital would care about drug deal-ers, but she was glad she wasn't dying, though not every part of her was convinced. The panic attacks lasted for a couple of years until she finally figured them out.

Losing air.

*Air!*

*Erich!*

*Er!*

*Air escaping from my chest—my heart.*

*My heart is broken.*

*He's dead to me.*

*I'm dying because he's gone.* She used to cover up the phantom holes with her tiny fingers, and when she took them off she would hear a *sssssssss* sound, feel the air. Even now, when she took a bus in New York City, the bus would sometimes make a sound that reminded her of that hissing, and she would sweat.

With Jonathan there was also pain, along with anger and resentment. She was no longer certain if she loved him and was beginning to wonder if she ever did. Over the years they had roughly agreed that they had different definitions of love and different operating systems. She didn't love him the way she wanted to—with a constant, open sensation in her chest—a heavy and warm link from her chest to his as she had experienced with Erich. But after he'd explained how he loved her: he cared for her, trusted her, loved being with her, respected her, thought she was beautiful and sexy and wanted to be with her and make her happy, she realized she felt the same way. She loved him on his terms—with his terminology.

Something was right about this and something was just plain dumb. At the level of formal logic it all made sense. Through the symbolic order of language they were even. But wasn't love an intentional state, as she learned in her philosophy days? It wasn't at all about *sign*, it was about *signified*.

Once, pointing to her heart, she asked, "Do you feel something here?"

"Yes, Sarah," Jonathan said unconvincingly.

"No, really," she said. "Not metaphorically. I mean, does your heart beat faster, say, when you think of me or look at me?"

Jonathan's desire to be truthful beat his deeper need to construct a lie that could maybe keep her in a way he didn't feel he had her. "Well, no. No I don't feel anything there."

"Well, if you're interested, that's love on my terms," she told him.

"That's not love for me," he said.

*Maybe some people have deeper capacities for love—can feel more intensely*, she began to think. She was passionate and fiery and was now experienced enough to believe that she couldn't expect to have those college-day sensations forever.

"You can't sustain the kind of passion that you had with Erich for long," her old friends told her. "If you had a love like that in a marriage you'd be dead." She wondered how many movies that year she had seen with the same premise. Anyway, what did they know, these friends who had happily left their Vassar men to meet her to discuss Erich when he wasn't around? They didn't get it.

Had she settled? Maybe . . . but at least consciously, knowing that this love with Jonathan was in fact the only kind of love she could live with for years—cliché or not.

The computer was Sarah's center now and every night she hoped she'd hear from Erich. A week had gone by since her e-mail to him and her heart raced when she saw his address in her In-box. She opened it:

Dear Sarah, and I mean dear,
So lovely to hear from you.

For the record: I did love you. I never lied—not about that. But I was a prick, you know. I do not remember the incident on the stairs, though I am sure I thought I was being amusing when I said, "I like you, too." You

were a beautiful girl—incredible. I know I hurt you
when I left you for Isabella. I was young. I do remember
coming to your room and telling you I didn't love her,
and it was true. I'm glad you have written me after so
long. I have thought about you over the years, figured
you were married with children. Am I right?

As for your prose: I was critical of you because I saw a
great potential in you. I am sorry for any pain I may
have caused you. Your fragments are lovely. As for
Oxford, I am amusing myself with a tenure track in
these hallowed, dusty halls of Philosophy.

Regards,
Erich

That serious exchange between them was the beginning
of some very smart and flirty, ambiguously erotic e-mails.
The kind that had Sarah wishing she slept alone so that she
could touch herself where she pleased and think only of Erich
and his wit. Kissing him down there, smelling him. There
was plenty of guilt, of course.

After a couple of months, the virtualness of it finally became more than she could bear. She wanted to touch him,
really touch him. She needed to. His good mind distracted
her and pulled her. Never mind that Jonathan was sensing
something: a missing-Sarah in the bed at two in the morning,
every night.

She wrote: *E—I'm going to be in town for a conference from
the 13th to the 21st. I'd love to see you. Will you be around? —
S.*

Because there wasn't a conference, she figured she would

go to a few museums, and if things went well with him, would tell him the truth—that she was there for him.

And then there was Jonathan. She was lying to him, too. She barely even told him about the "conference," and he was barely interested. At least, that's what she thought.

Days later, Erich replied: *I would love to see you. Do you need a fat? You can stay with me, if you want.*

"A *fat?*" she said out loud to herself. "That's some typo." He had always been rotten about her fleshy parts—calling her a "heffalump" at his most endearing. She was round, it's true, but she was beautiful. Back then she looked like an auburn Breck girl with dirty hair. But Erich, ever the misogynist, didn't care for tits and ass in those days—the anorectic aesthetic was in vogue then, and it tapped his homoerotic, pedophilic, ascetic nature.

⁓

At their small, upstate international airport, Sarah sat at gate three expectantly.

She was thinking about Erich. His creativity, the way he put words together, the way he understood the world, it all made her wet. He had his own ideas about things. He was an original thinker. A philosopher. And she had loved him so much, she had never really stopped loving him. Toe or no toe. All right, so he was a little amoral and nihilistic. And violent. But she missed that feeling of looking up to him. Or having an equal to share her ideas with. She missed her feelings. Yes, Jon was great in many ways, a great father, she told herself, but he lacked "the creative," and a deep sense of self.

Her cell phone rang. She put a pen in *Brain's End*, the novel she was reading.

"Hello?"

"Hi. I'm at the airport. Where are you?" She was silent with guilt. It was Jon.

". . . Um, Virgin, terminal B, gate three. What are you doing here? Is everything all right?" she said.

"Everything's fine. I'll be right over."

Sarah had only a few minutes to feel sick and think. Jon was there sooner than she thought he'd be.

"Hi, Sarah," he said, sitting down on the ledge near the window, across from her.

"Everything's okay?" she asked again.

"Yeah, yeah . . . everything is fine . . ."

"Well, what are you doing here, then?" she asked.

"I came to see you off to your conference. I know you like being alone at the airport, but I wanted to talk to you. We haven't been talking much and . . ."

"Oh, oh . . ." Sarah was stunned and feeling a bit nauseated. Was it the falafel? No, it was Jon.

"Well, that's really . . . it's really nice . . . but weird. Something's up . . . I mean, this is stranger than this novel," she said, showing him the book she was reading.

"I just missed you. I didn't feel like we had a good goodbye and I wanted to talk, face to face. No cell phones."

"That's very sweet, Jon . . ." she said.

"So, tell me about this conference again. Are you . . . you haven't really told me anything about it," he said.

"I tried to. You didn't seem interested. I told you, it's the International Science Writer's Guild, remember?—it's about unifying the social sciences and—"

"You're right, I don't care. Why didn't you tell me you were staying with *Erich?*" he said.

"How do you—?"

"I read your e-mails. And it's bullshit, Sarah. Isn't it? There's no conference. I checked."

"You checked? How do you *check* something like that?"

"I did my best. I'm a pretty good researcher."

"Well, you're right, there's no conference, but you shouldn't have read them. Jesus, Jon!"

"You're not the one to be talking about 'shouldn't,' Sarah!"

"But, you shouldn't have read them, it's not right."

"All is fair in—!"

"I'm sorry . . ." she said.

"I don't think you should go. . . . Please don't go Sarah, please. . . ." he said.

"Look, this is the first time in a decade I'm doing something I want to do—need to do! Whatever this desire is, it's bigger than me and if I don't act on it—it's the death of me. Without desire I may as well not exist. I may as well just be dead."

"Sarah, why do you have to be so damn melodramatic? Look, when I married you it was—well, you remember our vows—I thought you thought the same. . . ." he said pathetically, not even attempting *the death of desire is the death of the individual* meme.

"I did. Jonathan—"

"I don't want to stand in your way of happiness, for Christ's sake, Sarah! But is Erich the answer here? This sounds like a destructive impulse. . . . Everything you've told me about him—I don't want you to go—I'm afraid he'll hurt you . . ."

"Jon. Stop. Just stop! I'm going. It's what I want to do. I care about you—I do. And I know this hurts—on all sorts of levels." She needed to keep the door open a little and he was happy to let her. "Look, this is very difficult, I know. What can I say? I feel terrible. Rotten. Selfish. Hurtful. But if I don't do this you may as well be married to an amoeba. I need time. And I need to explore my feelings."

"You're a beautiful amoeba," Jonathan said, but was thinking, *I know what you need to explore, that damn German prick!*

"Jon, I don't think you get it. And that's probably one of our problems. I'm sorry, Jon. I'm going. . . . But can I tell you something sort of dopey . . . something I've been thinking about. . . ?

"Of course. A baby theory?" he said, tenderly.

"Well, it's more like a prenatal theory," she said smiling.

And he laughed a little. They were feeling really grownup.

". . . It's this pattern with me . . . three stages I go through, over and over again," she said.

"What is it?"

"Well, the first is birth, where we go toward the world; the second, life, where we push up against it, resist it, fight it—to feel it, to define what it is, who we are; and the third is death, where we go away. . . . That's the way it feels I go through life. I go toward people and things and love them and want to be loved. Then I fight them, resist them, feel anger, in order to define, understand. And then I retreat, pull back . . . to finally emerge after 'death' with some self-knowledge or understanding, only to start again. A reincarnation of the self."

"I see. So that's what you're hoping for with this? I don't know what to say. I just don't want you to go," he said.

"I know. I'm sorry . . . they're boarding my row, though— I'm gonna go."

Jonathan smiled and gave a small wave. He headed for the men's room and sobbed in a stall.

☙

After eleven days of feeling young and alive, she returned to New York. On the plane she sat fantasizing and remembering her time with Erich: Eating at the pub on the corner. Fucking on his bathroom floor. Coffee and cigarettes in bed first thing in the morning. Sex in the bookstore, on the tube out to the gardens. They couldn't keep their hands and mouths off and out of each other. She lost and found herself and it was good. Really good. "My dick is so hard for you, Sarah." "Your pussy's so sweet and welcoming," he'd say. She never needed foreplay, she was always wet for him. And he loved that about her. He loved knowing whenever he wanted her, he could just go into her. "I find it a brilliant attribute in a woman when she is agreeable," he had said.

He had only roughed her up a bit once, and it didn't hurt. He had thrown her up against the wall in frustration—his own about himself.

They were supposed to have met for coffee, not tea, at a café in Kensington. He never made it and he never called her cell phone—didn't answer *his*. She felt like she was repeating the same old patterns with him, but she couldn't get out of it. Why did the anger at his not showing excite her sexually? It seemed counterintuitive to her that the emotion of betrayal should be linked to her vulva. She wanted to sever that nerve that connected mind and body (and heart?). It was an unnecessary link. It made more sense from an evolutionary standpoint that *trust* would make her amorous, desirous, open. Perhaps in the reorganization of her brain, after all the deaths she had experienced, a connection went awry. But then it happened. The cut. The Cartesian cut.

She was in his Kensington flat asking him why he never showed up, why he never called. And he was a shit about it. He told her he had to meet a friend who needed to talk, and "Sorry," he didn't have time to call. And they fought about this. Until her face was in his hands very tightly, her head against the wall. Until her heart was racing from fear. And then bang!, his fist on the wall, right next to her face, his other hand gripping her chin and cheek. Bang! His groin against her, pressing.

And then he let go. And she slid . . . down the wall's

smooth, cool surface, crumpling herself into a numb dustball on the floor. She wasn't *hurt*. (He had only hit the wall.) What she was, was *saved*. Because she didn't want anymore; she felt nothing. No stirrings in her groin. No feelings in her heart. And she was sort of shocked at the loss of feeling. It was bittersweet.

Looking out the window on the plane, she felt pangs of feeling and regret for Erich, numbness, and perhaps also love.

He was back in her toe.

She wrote in her journal:

When you're eighteen and a woman, it's easy to imbibe the cultural ethos that you're shit. Is it that we disdain pure potential? The young woman as empty vessel—yearning to be filled: with men, babies? It was too easy getting smacked around by a sociopath who did smack more than he ate. I thought I deserved it. I craved romantic experience. But I've got too much experience now and I no longer think I'm shit. Maybe I was so numb from Mom and Dad and Sally and Grama that I required pain to feel anything at all. I just wanted to feel. And feel I did. I felt it when he made my lip bleed, and for all my logorrhea, I cannot put in words—the euphoric—no—orgiastic—no!—it was like the heavy tension felt between two magnets with the same charge—that invisible but weighty feeling which should repel but which compels, which pulled me in deeper.

I have to think of Maggie now. I chose to marry Jonathan for many reasons. I loved him and love him as much as I could and *can* love a best friend. He is a good father. And he is a good model for Maggie. I want her to be able—from the beginning—without struggle, to love a man who will be good to her. I don't want to perpetuate the alpha-desiring lineage. It must be broken. It's a sacrifice I make for my descendants. The will is stronger than the heart.

She took out her laptop and, looking back on her notes in her blue Florentine book, began a scene in *Chimeras* or *Supermen,* she wasn't sure which, about Sylvia, a human female who falls in love with Dionysus, an atavistic superman, a superman *with* desire:

Love and sex had always been the same for Sylvia. She had never been able to separate them. It seemed that men always could, quite successfully. Love here. Sex there. This time she would try to get at the heart through sex. A back door. She had no choice. Because he was like an express teleport whose doors closed fast. If she didn't jump on, she'd lose her ride.

And then Sarah remembered Nietzsche: "One does not get over a passion by representing it: rather, it is over when one is able to represent it." She wasn't sure if she agreed. She knew she had a way to go but she was almost there. Regardless, she knew her place was in Windhover with Jonathan and the children, having realized what she already suspected about hot love and warm love. Both were lethal to her in some way, but she decided to be an adult, and so live and die with a man she loved gently and who was the father of her children and who loved her softly, too.

Jonathan was in the living room when Sarah returned. The children were still at camp, thank god, and Jon and Sarah could begin to repair the damage. He went into the bedroom to get the gift his brother, Hadyn, had given him. He brought it downstairs, aimed it at Sarah, and whispered, "I loved you."

Then he aimed it at himself and pulled the trigger.

It wasn't loaded. He had never bothered to check it. He had been afraid of it, actually. They stared at each other and then Jonathan broke down. "I love you," she consoled.

And though they both knew it was his kind of love, they soon forgot.

*red love*

And I want an elevating love.
—*Caleb Matthews*

# *red*

That was the story Sullivan read on the computer; the story Karina wrote.

This is how it came to be written. This is how it came to be read:

There is a phenomenon train riders know well called sac-cade. Without will, the central foveal area of the retinal field detects an object—a *saccadia*—and then another. Karina watched this changing of focus from one point to another as she rode the number one train south. She watched as the passengers' eyes danced involuntarily left, right, left, right—their eyes catching the large station numbers on the tiled walls— 103, 96, 86, 79—as the subway sped out of the stations.

Between stops their eyes focused elsewhere. Karina imagined their lovers, their sadnesses, the dinners awaiting them, and she was egalitarian about them: the attractive ones caught her attention, but she also scanned for the average, the flashless. The twenty-seven-year-old woman with three kids, no husband and two jobs, wanting love. A fifty-nine-year-old janitor with one son in jail, a daughter with HIV, and who, just a week before his retirement, is fired because someone accused him of stealing a computer at the school. Of course, he didn't do it.

She watched mostly those unlike her, those who weren't watching—the readers, the dozers, and her favorite, the unselfconscious subway primpers. Those who used the IRT for personal care were a strange lot. She had seen women put on too much makeup, saw a pretty Asian woman pluck tiny hairs from her face, saw a man brandish a pocket knife and use it to cut his fingernails, and once witnessed, horror of horrors, a man in a business suit floss his teeth.

Though her focus was mindful, there were times when even the fair Karina could not help herself. At a restaurant, say, with Sullivan, she might suddenly become uncomfortably aware that she was staring at a woman who sparkled, showed skin, or whose trip to the bathroom revealed a large, pantilined bottom through too tight pants. These sights stood out in the visual field despite others there who, if she thought about it, were more attractive and interesting—more aesthetically sympatico. She recognized, through catching herself watch these saccadias, these women with ample asses, low cut dresses and shine, that if this worked on her, it must work on men more so, on every level, and at all times. Whereas for her it was a visual atavism, an old deep reflex, she figured with Sully it was deeper but also closer to consciousness; it took up all his layers.

The world she created for the handsome man diagonal to her on the local was altogether different from the world he created for her. She imagined he was a Wall Street executive, Princeton raised and schooled who couldn't commit to his longtime girlfriend and who was so tight with his money and affection he'd never be happy. It wasn't exactly the world he created for her, *saccadia*, par excellence. He saw her in a black teddy with her leg up on a bed. No. His bed. He held her breasts, got her from behind, and when he was done she conveniently had to go.

Karina had thought about getting off at 72nd Street to wait for an express but decided to stay on the local. When she got to 42nd Street the express was across the tracks. She stood up and stood in the doorway of the car. She wondered if the express was about to pull out of the station. She couldn't tell. She didn't want to run across the platform only to have the express doors close on her, only to have to turn around and have the local doors close on her to be left without a ride. It had happened before. It wouldn't happen again, she decided, and sat back down.

Saccade again. Eyes dancing back and forth, focus changing reflexively, automatically, without intention. And finally, 14th Street. She stood up as Mr. Princeton gazed upon her, rehearsing his fantasy, and a bit sadly, exited the closing doors, leaving the folks with hard lives, and bounded up the stairs to 12th Street. On the corner of 8th Avenue she rang the buzzer of an old warehouse. She peered into the conspicuous camera and was buzzed in to ISO headquarters.

These were strange, quiet times for the International Socialist Organization, indeed for all American socialists and communists. There was no Soviet Union. And the American youth, long cherished by the left, were at best apathetic, if not conservative. Most of the radicals who managed to get through the apolitical me-decade eighties were too politically depressed in the years after, and many sympathetically abandoned the movement.

Karina supported and associated herself not only with ISO; she flirted with the SWL (Socialist Workers League), the ICP (International Communist Party), and the TP (Trotskyist Party). Though there must have been dozens of small leftist groups, these were the ones Karina decided stood a chance of changing the world. And she was uniquely popular with them all. She was coveted like their golden girl, like she was Marilyn Monroe entertaining the troops. Karina was, for these old Marxists, their muse—their inspiration to fight the good fight; she got their sanguine juices flowing.

It wasn't her intellect that moved them (perhaps some even wished she were less smart and critical), or her position on Yugoslavia, the former Soviet Union or her extensive knowledge of the thirties' labor movement in America. It was that they wanted her, to possess her, to have her in their party—their poster girl. They wanted to see the beautiful Karina holding their sign saying *GM Workers Unite! Pick off the Scabs! Organize with Labor! For an Internationalist Workers Party!* They wanted her because they knew people believed in beauty. Because *they* believed in beauty.

The truth is, the men in these organizations could not stop talking about her. They wanted to recruit her or seduce her, or both. (They knew about Sullivan but his existence didn't seem to stop their fantasies.) And the women talked about her, too—and not just the lesbians. In fact, the straight women did most of the talking—maybe so they wouldn't feel bad when the men did or to show the men they didn't care or weren't intimidated. It was the alpha girls of the parties who had the hardest time with Karina. In the first place, she was at least ten if not fifteen years these girls senior—it hurt their young commie egos not to be able to keep the men's attention with their infant flesh alone.

But it wasn't simply Karina's beauty that captured the fantasy lives of so many Bolsheviks in New York City. Karina was elusive. She would not be recruited and this made her desirability staggering. She was on every red's mind all the time.

She figured, *what's the use of giving my life up to one marxist group if there's no chance of class struggle?* She vowed that she'd support them, go to meetings, fund-raisers, and demonstrations, and if the time came and she was needed for important revolutionary work, she'd join. But it wasn't her style to belong to just one group. Why the SWL and not the ISO? The factions and splinter groups were dizzying and imperfect: One group had great leadership but treated its women comrades miserably, another had great political positions but annoying and prickly party members.

*How does the damn Democratic Party do it? Why can't we just have one left party in this country? Our derision has led to our destruction,* she had thought. She understood there were real political differences and why they were important; she just saw them as barriers to achieving what they all wanted: equality for blacks and other minorities, including women, the poor. Decent lives for everyone—not just in America but worldwide. To end human suffering.

Despite her beauty, Karina was not self-conscious the way other beautiful women were. One got the impression she didn't know, though she had to, or if she knew, didn't care. But she *was* self-conscious of her ancestry. She was part Scot, part First People. She had Native American blood—sort of injected into her. The First Peoples of Onondaga, known as the People of the Hills, had stolen some of her recent ancestors in an act that left the family shattered and fragmented. Her great-great-great-grandmother was kidnapped along with two of her children, a daughter, Sylvia, and son, William, leaving her great-great-great-grandfather to raise Jacob, Samuel and Rebecca. Years later, after Sylvia's mother had died, she and her Indian family visited the town from which she was stolen. She found her sister, Rebecca, married but childless. On the day of Sylvia's return to her Indian village, she gave Rebecca a gift. Her name was Ewanni. She was Rebecca's niece and would later be called Frances. And though she was beautiful—she looked like a Tibetan princess—many in the town talked about the "half-breed," and though most understood why Rebecca kept her, no one could understand why Sylvia gave her.

Karina felt injustice in her blood. Within her she felt the injustice of her people, those who had been massacred and whose land had been taken from them, but also the injustice against her white family—who had also been taken. So it was that every wrong in the world, she *felt,* and this affected her glorious and healthy constitution.

At the ISO meeting, Karina sat on the old couch listening to the bearded brilliance of her comrades. They spoke every word for her. Every hard line, every polemic, was a seduction. But she didn't feel right. It felt like a plant was growing in her throat, so she left the meeting early and watched saccade all the way home.

It was April but the city was brutally hot. Whatever virus Karina had now seemed to cross the safe borders of her skin, infecting the world around her: Sullivan, the house, her relationships. For three days she would answer the phone with a fever. And in the evenings confess to Sullivan how she hurt Paul West, Louise Grosset or Harry Schafsma's feelings and how rotten she felt about it. Sully tried to keep her from the phone. But Karina had a need to form and keep connections. She couldn't let a virus stand in the way of maintaining relationships, after all. And so her actions reflected this social desire, but her words didn't.

Maybe it was the fever, or free-floating anger—the kind that is native to us all. Or maybe it *was* specific and related to Sam, or Sullivan, or that C she got as an undergrad in her freshman seminar class with that right-wing professor. Or maybe it was what was just native to her. Whatever the cause, she hadn't the strength or will of restraint. The virus had perforated that essential filter that gets most of us through the day—the social one. And hers was a sieve with large holes to begin with.

To her friend Louise she had been particularly cruel. About Gregory, her adopted son from Romania with the behavioral problem, she had said: "C'mon, what do you expect? Do you really think Gregory can go from an orphanage where he probably got no more than twenty minutes of attention a day in miserable conditions to an abusive foster family, back to the orphanage and then to you—a depressed, neurotic, forty-three-year-old single mom who can't keep a job or finish her dissertation—*without* having problems? If he *wasn't* fucked up by all that there'd really be something wrong with him." She said this with some humor in her voice but Louise knew very well Karina meant every word and that she was probably right.

And then there was this conversation:

Lauren: I love him still. I'm in love with him.

Karina: Then why did you dump him, Lauren?

Lauren: You know why. Ultimately, he couldn't get serious. Elizabeth thinks I was really strong to be able to do that.

Karina: You know what I think? In complete Eros there is
   no Will to Power. In Will to Power there is no Eros.
Lauren: What does *that* mean?
Karina: If you really loved him you wouldn't break up
   with him just because he wouldn't settle down.
   You'd keep hoping that he would. If you truly
   loved him, you'd be compelled to do anything to
   keep him. You're not in love with him.
Lauren: Karina, let's talk when you're feeling better,
   okay? I'm really upset about this now.

Karina was fascinated with this topic—more than she said,
because she wasn't well and because talking never afforded her
the time to get at what she really wanted to, like her writing
did. She knew people were fundamentally interested in their
own story, the details of it—less in the meta-ness of it. But
she wondered, *What finally makes the less desired one, abandon ship? Is there a chemistry, a physics, a mathematics to it? Is
it from strength or weakness? And why are there those who never
leave, no matter what?*

When she was better, she would think she was forgiven by
her friends and colleagues because she was interesting and honest
and vital—passionate about her students, about social change,
and about life. But what probably saved her was her beautifully
round, sonorous laugh, mixed with an aesthetic ambrosia: her
perfect milk skin, almond eyes and honey-wheat hair that made
men want to take her home—because she actually lost Louise
and almost Lauren. The lesson *she* would take home: don't answer the phone when you're sick. But she'd do it again.

It seemed Karina's abundance of energy was reserved only for
lecturing friends and Sully during her sickness. Anything else was
too much: cleaning dirty, three-day-old dishes—some having never

made it to the sink, including her paternal grandmother's eighteenth-century English peony plates, which had glued to them, perhaps forever, the Chinese food she had eaten before she got sick, picking up "papers"—those damn papers that she often hounded Sullivan about—memos, receipts, magazines, messages, bills, empty envelopes, his work—everywhere.

Sullivan worshipped her. Sure, they had been fighting a lot but who didn't fight? He was tense working on his doctoral degree—the academic politics were more than he had bargained for even with his progressive milieu. He had been with pretty women all his life but never a woman whose beauty made men stutter or silent. She had had that kind of affect on him when they first met. He was looking for a roommate. He listed his share with Columbia's off-campus housing office and put signs on the street lamps and bus shelters along Broadway. He got a dozen and a half calls, and from those calls met about eight of them. When Karina walked into the apartment Sully was stunned. What was she doing looking for a roommate? *Why hadn't she been swept up by some exceedingly wealthy businessman or Hollywood executive? Couldn't someone like this be a model or an actress? She's an English professor and wants to share my place and sleep in the living room?*

His friends told him it was a terrible idea to live with a woman who made him weak and who he said he thought he might already love. And he had only several months ago broken up with Abby. He wasn't thinking straight, his friends told him. But he offered the living room to her and in two months they were both in the bedroom.

*Sure, things have slowed down in bed,* he was thinking to himself, and the fighting had steadily increased, but he knew that was fairly typical when you lived with someone. He expected it. He had no doubts about their relationship—he figured they'd marry after his Ph.D. in history and have kids. She'd be in her late thirties—she'd fit in perfectly with the other mothers he saw strolling babies on Broadway. But maybe Karina didn't feel this way. Every fight took away something for her—maybe feeling. *Maybe she doesn't feel what I feel,* Sully was starting to think.

Sully was no longer helping out. His energies, although boundless, were confined to one area or project in his life. In the heady days just a couple of years back with Karina, everything else fell to the side. But now his project was renovating a three-bedroom apartment on West End Avenue to which he devoted all his energies, and this somehow translated to a light touch in domestic areas.

Karina was beginning to fear that it was Sully's perfect, beautiful rent-controlled, pre-war, one-bedroom on Riverside Drive that kept them together when it seemed nothing else would. The apartment's lease had been his uncle's—a barrel of a man and Johnsonian Professor of History at Columbia. Uncle Sullivan and Sully shared the same name—Sullivan T. McCoy—which enabled Sully to take over the place when Uncle Sullivan left Morningside Heights for a better life and a better deal at Harvard.

Karina's non-tenured teaching salary at City College was decent but not enough for her to get a studio that was half as nice as Sully's eight hundred-square-foot spread. (Comparable one-bedrooms would cost more than double what they paid for the place.) And Karina realized that although Sully could arguably find another roommate, he or she would have to sleep in the living room. And since he had now lived with a living room without someone's life in it (bed, dresser, body, personal affects) for two years, Karina knew he'd prefer living with her and one bed in disharmony than with the alternative.

One of their problems, it seemed to Karina, was that for

many months, their fighting had degenerated into passionless banter and worse: right in the middle of an argument, either Karina or Sullivan would ask to end it. To her, this was contrary to universal laws of arguments, which boil and boil rapidly, effortlessly, and hard—until something happens—someone runs out of the apartment and the other chases; someone cries and the other consoles; someone apologizes and the other accepts; someone, in this case, Sully, bangs his fist on a door and it busts open—*not* the door; or the fight slows down from hours and hours of exhaustion until there's a stalemate and both forgive and forget. But asking in the heat of an argument for a cease fire? It was an unnatural conclusion, a forced consequence that went against her literary and philosophical sensibilities. But mostly it went against her passionate and stubborn nature, and it bothered her deeply.

But she was as guilty as Sullivan. She also had become enervated by the arguments and could no longer keep them going. *Better to end them sooner and save some energy for grading papers*, she'd think. She feared it meant they no longer thought each other was worth the effort, but she hoped it was because they were working too hard—and because they had been together just over the two year mark where evolutionary psychologists say the love chemicals peter off and the commitment molecules set in. Perhaps this new style of argumentation was good, she told herself. It was natural. It followed the logic of the sexes throughout evolution. The hot emotions of love and passion produce intense arguing, the cool feelings of respect and commitment urge you to stop: Get on with feeding babies, making weapons, hunting, gathering, bonding with other tribes—grading papers.

Karina had been feeling the mind-body dialectic problem for a while. Not really the philosophical one so much as the one which relates to her and men. She felt it was only her outward beauty that Sully was magnetized to. But he didn't seem to get *her*. He seemed to hate her intensity and passion. He wasn't that interested in her ideas, either. It felt like a waste. And she sort of didn't feel loved. Most any man could love her face, her body, but the man who loved the fire in her, the burst of memes in her, the artist in her . . .

Sullivan was a good man and she valued that. But she hated herself for not valuing it enough. It's like both had an abundance of qualities which the other ultimately wasn't turned on by. And yet, the contradiction was, they both needed those qualities.

She imagined a conversation with her colleague, Paul West, also an English professor at City College:

"Do you know Nietzsche's *Birth of Tragedy*?" she asks.

"Sure," he says.

"I've got this student who used it in his paper on Sophocles. He didn't get it right but it's interesting—"

She's cut off in her own fantasy.

"What is it . . . Dionysus versus Appolinian?"

"Yes—the Dionysian."

"Yes, right," he says. "Dionysian: irrational, overflowing, intoxicated, voluptuous, destructive. The Appolinian: rational, imagistic, and creative. In art, the Dionysian is music, the Appolonian, paintings, drawings . . . Right?"

"Yes. And within the classification of Dionysian art— music—there is a continuum of the Dionysian and Appolonian. Which do you think I'm more like?" she asks.

"Probably both. That's usually the answer to questions of dualism, right?" he says.

"Tell me more. . . ."

"Well, on the outside you are definitely Dionysian. It's your job to deconstruct—language—and papers."

"Deconstructing language makes me Dionysian?" she says.

Like a dream where the players change in the middle of the action in a kind of morphing, she now imagined the conversation was taking place with Sullivan:

"No, Kar. I was just kidding. But really, you're about breaking down walls, right?—politically and artistically—even if you're not always successful. And your drinking—"

"Wait, wait, wait—I asked a philosophical question here and you're on to me about drinking!"

She was kidding, she really wasn't feeling defensive, but this was typically lost on Sullivan, even in her daydream.

"I'm not on to you. Okay, on the inside, though, of this teeming sexual, hot, voluptuous, irrational woman there is an Appolinian impulse—a need to create and to build and to give life and meaning to things. Your stories. And you want children. Some revolutionary!"

"And you're both, too, I now see. Look what you do—construction, you build stuff. And history (Sully was a carpenter by trade but a Ph.D. candidate at Columbia by fate—all the men in his family and one aunt were historians—a few were marxists): it's analytical, ordered, rational, and you are a costructivist, aren't you?"

"Touché."

"But inside you know you have to deconstruct to build, and I know what pleasure you get in ripping stuff down. And once you were talking about Spain and you said in your most revolutionary and innocent way, 'Sometimes you need a revolution to create a better world,' and I told you then—surprise, surprise—that you were right."

"But revolution is not my impulse. Creating a better world is and it has been necessary for—"

"Okay, okay. Let's not get into this. We're both Appolinian and Dionysian."

It was her musing, so she had the last word.

It's frightening, but Karina truly had daydreams like this. It scared her, too. She had read somewhere that men have sexual fantasies nine times a minute. *If only I were a man,* she thought. Her fantasies were socio-logos-centered—in a word, Appolinian. Her fantasy life was limited to imagined conversations (political, literary, philosophical), imagining people's lives and her own acts of heroism. They were a precursor to her stories. If only she could imagine Paul or Harry in bed, or that sexy, new guy in the ICP who looked like Ed Burns— she'd be a lot happier, she knew. But the Dionysian wasn't flowing; her guilt saw to that.

Karina was starting to feel better. She was slowed down and well enough in this twilight between illness and recovery that she was able to take long, hot baths with lavender and chamomile. She could fantasize. And she could write. To piece stories together until she was all right in her mind and body.

She was well enough to read an article in the Sunday *Times Magazine* called "Save Sigmund Freud: What We Can Still Learn from a Discredited, Scientifically Challenged Misogynist." She read:

Because we both wish and oppose our own desires, our inner lives are in a constant state of civil war. What Freud taught us to do was to recognize the signs of that war and to see when it was reaching destructive imbalance. He let us know how we're likely to behave when desire slips loose from its reigns, but he also told us the price of too much prohibition. When the inner censor grows too strong, prohibits too much, the result is listlessness, depression, despondency. In extreme cases we reach acedia, the hatred of life that takes one to suicide. *The death of desire is the death of the individual.*

It was impossible for Karina to read the word suicide and not think of Sam. She lay back in her bed and thought of the last time she saw him and about how fooled he had had everyone. She hadn't known—no one knew—the kind of pain he was in or why. Sam playing football. Sam at the prom with the girls with big hair. Sam, the eternal yes-sayer, or so she had thought. It had been fourteen years since Sam had killed himself up at SUNY Oswego. A premeditated drug overdose. He left a three-page letter to his friends and family. Mostly the letter dealt with his possessions and where and to whom they should go. Their brother Joe got his prized comic book collection; Karina got his journals, of which there were many. She tried to read them when she came home for the funeral her senior year at Stonybrook. But Karina and Sam had been terribly close. And when she picked up those notebooks she felt the life in them. She felt his energy pass into her fingertips, up her arms, and down her spine. The intensity of her feelings, the crying and wailing, surpassed anything she had ever witnessed on television, on film or on stage. Art and culture betrayed her. It didn't prepare her; it didn't reflect her torment. And it was because her pain seemed so outside the normative values and understanding of culture that she worried about the depth of her feeling. And she was told often enough she wasn't normal. *It's not normal to be raw four years after the death of a brother*, someone once told her, blindly.

At first, Karina put the inherited journals in his room under his bed. He had kept them in his closet. And sometimes when she was home in Oswego at Christmas she would try to read them with her mother, but they both feared the notebooks would interrupt what little healing had begun. There was never a good time to read the *Logos* of your dead brother. One year she brought the journals back to the city with her, and stored them from apartment to apartment.

It had taken her almost five years for her to be able to go into the room Sam shared with Joe, their older brother, for any length of time. And when she was finally able to go in she'd sit in the middle of the floor holding something—a high school biology book that he never returned, a picture of one of the many girls he had dated. And then she'd go into their small bathroom and open the old medicine cabinet. She'd look at all the soaps, medicines, and general toiletries and wonder why her mother hadn't thrown them all away. She'd take down his shaving cream and squeeze foam out as big, fat tears rolled down her too thin cheeks. *How can this still be here and not you?* she'd say aloud, gazing past the worn, milky mirror, through her reflection, past sensory impressions, to the other side of the looking glass, hoping to find him. Many, many years later, she'd perform her ritual at the medicine cabi- net, and think, *old smelly shaving cream, way past its expira- tion, it wasn't supposed to last longer than Sam, it doesn't have a right to last this long.* She hated Gillette.

It was in Sully's apartment, in an old milk crate, at the back of the hall closet, that the answer or answers to Sam's desperate act might finally be found. She felt ready. She wasn't raw. She felt healed on the top layers. And she was smart enough to be prepared not to find answers. Now, during this strange free-time, between *bedridden* and *work,* which she equated with the time spent at airports, she'd finally read them. It was Sully's earlier rummaging getting the air conditioner in the front closet which managed to bring the crate in front of her when she opened the closet door. She was eerily amused. If she ever fictionalized this, this moment would have to be cut. Too often life gave her per- fect, serendipitous occurrences that were too hokey, too unbe- lievable for fiction. Her life wasn't stranger than fiction, it was more fictiony than fiction—at least modern fiction.

After reading through most of them, Karina was inspired—compelled to write.

She wrote:

*The artist must have something to say, for mastery over
form is not his goal but rather the adapting of form to its
inner meaning.*
*—Kandinsky*

What gaps do I leave? How much to give to the
reader? When is it too much? Not enough? It's like
seduction. Too much—it's obscene. Too little—not
enticing. How to give enough flesh so they want more?
And what do I want to do? I want to:

Draw the reader in—like a friend sitting down at a coffee
shop eager to hear the news of a new romance—or affair.

Heal the reader or give reader an *a-ha*, make reader
laugh, or think, or remember—give pleasure.

Use details and description sparingly, with meaning
and purpose.

Eschew dead, cliché phrases or metaphors. And if not,
use them correctly (e.g. begs the question). Conversely,
don't fear universals, like love, because they appear
unliterary.

Offer depth and layers and resonance for excavators
and detectives.

Be clear.

Be unpretentious and honest. Postmodern jargon
should neither hide a weakness to explain or describe,
nor cover up what is nonsense, weak, empty.

Have as many people read it as possible.

Be happy if it's only published in *Splinters*—or nowhere.

Write things people are afraid to say so that they can say them.

Because that's one of art's missions. It pushes us. It reveals. It pries us open little by little, exposing us, in a comfort zone. It's about normative values. And power, of course. The rulers of art are the true rulers. Forget about the means of production. Art changes the strategy of reproduction. We are the product of art. Our minds, our bodies. What cultural products are valued? Rejected? What survives? Who survives? Art throughout history— the progression and unfolding of it.

And then she wrote "soft kill."

Days later, she and Sully sat down to eat Indian take-out in front of *Entertainment Tonight* after his very long, hot day of ripping out molding and skim coating. Karina was feeling better and was full of energy and spice. She wanted to engage him in ideas, half-thought out ones, and Sully wanted a beer and a game.

"There are three kinds of people in the world," Karina said.

"Yeah? Do you know what channel MSG is on?"

"Twenty-nine or twenty-three. Do you want to hear my three kinds of people idea?"

"I'd rather watch the Yankees," Sully said wryly, thinking his audience would not take offense. He dialed around for a while and returned to *Entertainment Tonight*, defeated and miserable.

"A King Fisher would really be good right now but I'd settle for anything."

Karina went into the kitchen and grabbed a Rolling Rock for him.

"Here, Sul. Okay, so the idea is that there are three kinds of people: readers, writers and livers."

"Livers?" Sullivan said disgusted.

"Yes, livers—hold the onions. As in those who live—it *is* a word. I know it's not beautiful. I thought of 'lovers of life' instead—a sort of reference to Plato—and it sounds better, but it messes up the symmetry with 'writers' and 'readers.' Anyway, I'm sticking with livers. You may think of it as the 'lovers of life' if you want."

"All right, all right, you're going to lose me if you—hey, I found a game," he said, holding the remote in the air like it was a magic wand.

"Okay! Most people in the world are readers—passive, taking the world in, experiencing other people's experience or imagined experiences—watching TV is 'reading.' The writers (and one needn't write to fit into this category—it's more like a sensibility)—"

"Oh no?" Sully said ironically but with his interest piqued a bit at this seeming contradiction.

". . . are observers, reflective, they talk about experience, write about it, respond to it. The livers, are busy living so they're not writing or reflecting because they're caught up in the moment of their experience—living it. We're all probably all three at different points in our lives, at different times of the day. Observing, acting, reflecting."

"Okay, so I'm a *reader* obviously. And you? You're a liver, right?"

"I'm all three, but I guess I'm mostly a writer, unhappy being a reader, wishing I were a liver. I'm comfortable observing, reflecting, learning, responding—not as comfortable being passive, but I guess I want to live more. I want to live fully and feel fully. To be truly alive."

"You lost me there, Kar. That's the way I think of you, can't think of anyone more like that than you."

"I'm glad, at least I put on a good show for all you readers." Karina laughed, knowing she didn't have much longer before Sully lost interest. . . . She thought to herself, *I don't want to think when I'm doing. I want to lose myself. In the moment. To be pure—without self-consciousness, without thought.*

"You know, I think somehow those three modes of being must be similar to the three *gunas*—in Indian philosophy," she said.

"What's a *guna?* Sounds like something you put on nan bread."

"I suppose you could. But, *gunas* are the three modes of nature—*sattva:* goodness, *rajas:* passion, and *tamas:* dullness."

"Mmm, I'd like some *rajas* and maybe just a little *sattva*— hold the *tamas.*"

"I *bet* you would like a little *rajas.*"

"Can you pass the *raita?*" he said.

"Sure . . . here . . . but anyway, the three *gunas* are—"

"Wait, wait, shhh for a second, that's Tony Rivera—he hasn't struck out once this year and the pitcher—Gary Rodd— is the best there—shit, it's out—it's out of the park!! Hooo-hoeow. Okay, what was that, Kar?"

"That's okay," she said, "I was just going to go on about *gunas.* You'd rather hear about *aesthemiotics,* wouldn't you?"

"I don't know. I don't know what it is. . . . Aesthetics and semiotics?"

"Very good."

"What is it?"

"It's the aesthetic interpretation of signs and codes. The study of the phenomenon of beauty becoming its opposite. And the reverse—the ugly becoming beautiful. When an attractive signal becomes 'too loud,' 'grotesque,' how the signal loses its power from 'trying' too hard, how it becomes ugly."

"You lost me," he said. To be fair, he was trying to watch a game.

"Okay, think of anorexia. In anorexia, women's bodies are symbolic of the Nietzschean 'ascetic ideal,' which is fundamentally anti-grotesque. By demonstrating the ascetic ideal, the lack of excess and spectacle, she reaffirms excess—she becomes grotesque."

"You gotta give me something more than that postmodern crap!"

"Okay, Monsieur Foucault," she said. Sully had an annoying habit of acting disdainful of academia, when in fact, he was seriously in the muck of it. Maybe that's why.

"All right . . . a better example is the 'grunge' look. When we were in school, a decade before it was called 'grunge' it was a code, remember? For an abundance of resources and creative impulses—only a rich college kid or a kid with artistic talents could 'afford' to wear the 'sign' of torn leather and low, dirty jeans. There was beauty in the old and worn. It represented an emphasis on the interior. It was a reaction to the status symbol fashion—an exaltation of the poor. It was sort of Jesus-like. Spiritual. There's beauty in the strength of someone who doesn't care about her image. Behind the five dollar vintage dress with holes lies—we imagine—an inner beauty or talent or resource or strength. But with time, the sign becomes saturated. The look loses its meaning as it becomes popular, and counter reactions appear—a new code or signal."

Then she asked him to read her story. She was clearly pushing it.

"Forget it, Karina! Just about every time you've made me read one of your stories, I've ended up downtown all night with Gary, plastered, or you've gone down to Helen and Sasha's, or we've talked about your moving out. I don't want you to move. Anyway, you like it here too much. You like the views—you even sometimes like me."

"Humph!" Karina said. Sullivan grabbed the sports section of the *Times* and escaped to the bathroom. She followed him and despite herself stood outside the door unrelenting.

"Karina—I'm busy here!" Sullivan said, now angry. She opened the door part way.

"I thought you might find it interesting. . . . I just want a little feedback, Sul."

He threw down the paper. "Jesus Christ, Karina, you should leave me alone." She went back to *ET* and he joined her one segment on Johnny Depp later. Restraint was not her strong suit.

"If you're concerned it'll bring up issues—" Karina continued to hound Sullivan who now was concentrating undeliberately and unconsciously on a commercial with a lot of women's tan flesh. It was that degrading, campy beer commercial that poked fun at sexist beer commercials while all the while owning Sullivan's occipital lobe. On a moral and practical level, this irritated Karina to the point of frustration. But in the abstract, Karina enjoyed this about him. He was a handsome, hard working, enlightened academic who appreciated tits and ass as much as her brother Joe—an unenlightened UPS driver in Onondaga, New York—or her Uncle Dick, and her own father, both fishermen, did. Sullivan wasn't working class, but at least he shared some of their sensibilities. "Sully!" Karina jabbed.

"Sorry—what?" Karina could see she was beat.

Days later, Karina was better and back teaching. Having reread her story, she realized Sullivan was smart not to want to read it.

But Sully was in their bedroom at the desk with the computer on. He had a paper to write and was looking for distraction. Anything was better than: "The Era of NEP, 1921-1928: How does NEP bring ideological consistency to the revolution that was prematurely staged in November 1917?"

He started by looking around at all the pretty things Karina had about.

He gazed at the simple African-American quilt hanging on the wall; it was a Log Cabin quilt: red, orange, black, purple, brown, turquoise and yellow, with a black backing.

Karina loved that quilt. She had been turned on to quilts after reading Sue Bender's *Plain and Simple: A Woman's Journey to the Amish.* She became particularly interested in African-American quilts and often enough incorporated some piece of information about them into one of her classes. During sections on the Reconstruction period, she would explain how quilts were used as maps to freedom for members of the Underground Railroad. She'd bring in her own quilt and large picture books on African-American quilts to show them. The North star, crossroads, log cabin . . . all these patterns within the quilt represented a message, a signal. Karina loved this. Art as code and signal. Art as savior, as rescuer. She never felt badly that most of her students weren't that interested because it wasn't "cool." She knew they were busy weaving their own lives, looking for their own codes and signals—maps to freedom. But she always hoped that, despite their seeming apathy, the quilts would reach a place beyond cool and have some meaning for them.

Sullivan tried to remember what she had told him about these quilts. He remembered there was something about the black cloth on the back, but forgot what: that Log Cabin quilts with black cloth were hung to mark a safe house of refuge. And there was something about the patterns in the quilts and evil spirits. But he couldn't remember that either. What she had told him was that aside from the messages within the quilt, there was also significance in the patterns—particularly the breaks and changes in the patterns. Many African tribes believed that evil traveled in straight lines—so, the break or change was meant to confuse the evil spirits and slow them down. Wearing or having or creating this art symbolized a kind of rebirth, a kind of power.

He gazed at the beautiful antique etching of three women dressed in flowing gowns in the style of Tadema and Burne-Jones propped up on the desk. He studied it carefully. He had never noticed it before. One woman was at a spinning wheel. Another woman's hands were outstretched. The third woman held a pair of shears. They just looked like three beautiful women to him. They looked like Karina. But they were the three fates: *Clotho*, the spinner of the thread of life; *Lachesis*, the disposer of lots, assigning each person's destiny; and *Atropos*, the one who finally cuts the thread. He couldn't have known that. Actually, Karina hadn't known either. It was just something she found at an antique shop once.

Then his eyes went back to the computer. *NEP. NEP. Fuck NEP!* That "soft kill" icon on the desktop made him curious. He double-clicked on it and began reading about the memes, Jonathan's lack of focus on Sarah and her baby theories . . .

After he read it, he reread the last line: "And though they both knew it was his kind of love, they soon forgot."

Sully closed the document and sat there for a while looking at the blue screen and out at the river.

Karina came home and walked into the bedroom.

"I read 'soft kill,'" Sully said. And then a bit sadly, "It made me think about things. . . . You're going to leave, aren't you?"

And Karina said, with the lightness of a finch's wings, "Oh, Sullivan, it's just a story."

# *love*

I will rise now, and go about the city in the streets, and in
the broad ways I will seek him whom my soul loveth.
—*Song of Songs*

*Separation*
Your absence has gone through me
Like thread through a needle.
Everything I do is stitched with its color.
—*W.S. Merwin*

Karina wasn't teaching the whole summer. She planned it that
way. She taught an extra class at The New School (though her
main salary was coming from CCNY) and freelanced as a
copyeditor so she could afford the summer off. After all, there
was music to hear, political work to do, writing. She had finally
figured out that life was about pacing and that she was lousy at
it, and so she built, in a way, pacing into her life. She was like a
sprinter in a long-distance marathon race—she could finish with
the best of them, she just did it with fast dashes and breaks in

between. And she had earned this break. She had spent much of the year exhausted and weak after each class, pouring herself into each student, absorbing their family problems, their racist encounters, their young urban struggles.

Karina picked up a journal in Labyrinth, the local academic bookstore:

Dear Sarah (my beautiful and sad character in "soft kill," my alter-ego?),

Things with Sully are not good. I think it was the story. In some ways you are to blame. He says he loves me but I don't feel it, don't feel his love. I say I love him but I'm not sure that I do. If I can? I think maybe because I don't feel his love. I feel the hole I wrote you felt. I'm not sure if I feel anything. If I have for the longest time?

—K

Dear Sarah,

It's been a long time since my first and very last short entry. My handwriting even looks different. And you and I, we're that different, too.

I have a story for you. This one's real.

It was about five years ago, not long after my first and only entry, June and muggy and I was late for a party for the ICP down in the meat-packing district. It was to be a special one: Spearhead, Martin Sexton and The Green Thugs were performing a benefit concert for an old Black Panther on death row. More money was needed now for his legal defense as the judge in the '70s case had recently died and his wife came forward to say that he was a terrible racist and that he had confided to her that he knew the "nigger didn't do it." Many scorned her for not bringing it to someone's attention back then, others were impressed with her courage and decency, and still others—mostly folks in Queens—thought she was making it up. Anyway, old Ray Collins was going to get a fair trial this time—maybe.

I played back my messages:

"Karina, it's Paul. Need to talk about this CUNY open admissions demo. We're getting into some trouble with you know who. Call me back—"

"Hey, it's me. [It was Sullivan] Uh, I can't get over to the party—I'm going to be at the library for at least eight hours—gotta finish this paper. You'll probably be home before me. Okay? I'm sorry. I'll see you later. Bye."

Sometimes I liked going to parties by myself, but that night I wasn't up to it. When you don't have any energy sometimes all you need is another body next to you. I needed Sully's presence to prop me up like a ragdoll on a shelf—I was tired and pre-menstrual and it was the anniversary of Sam's suicide. I wasn't so sure I could carry on a conversation at all, let alone be intelligible or charming. Still, it was a good cause and I loved Michael Franti and Martin Sexton so I just made myself do it. I was hoping the music would heal me.

After I handed over my ticket at the door, I walked in to the huge factory/loft. It was dark and I couldn't make out much of anything at first. Then the faces became visible—NYU kids, hippies, straight-looking communists, undercover cops (they were the ones whose dress was a bit off—you weren't sure what they were but you knew they were trying to blend in—and they stupidly didn't talk to anyone), academics, lawyer types, the occasional leftist Hollywood celebrity. I said hello to some comrades and got a beer. The bartenders for the event were ICP people, of course, and mostly new. One was the Ed Burns look-alike. And I liked. Too much. I had finally allowed myself a sexual fantasy a week before that and it was about this guy who was now giving me a cold Bud. I was slightly embarrassed. Could he tell? I'm sure I blushed. We had never spoken before, probably because I avoided him. Not to be elusive or mysterious—I was just afraid there might be sexual tension that I couldn't handle. I didn't want to add trouble to my existent problems with Sully. It was my silly way too of being faithful. As if talking to this guy meant it would lead to sex!

The Ed Burns guy says in a lovely Irish accent, "Karina, Karina, you're unrecruitable I hear." We had never spoken before and the way he said my name with his mellifluous accent sucked me in more than his rugged, handsome face and mountain climber's body. It promised something different—foreign and sweet.

"Probably, yes, that may be true," I said, intrigued.

"So why do you think they bother then?" he asked wryly.

"You know communists—they love a challenge," I said.

"Yeah, *that's* true. Well, can you let *me* have a go at you then?"

"I beg your pardon?" My weariness was actually a plus that evening because it probably gave me an air of coolness I don't really have.

"Let me try to recruit you," he said.

"I don't even know your *name.*"

"Finn. Finn McCourt. No relation to that Pulitzer Prize winner. Well, maybe a long time ago. When can I recruit you?"

I was starting to think that *recruit* was a civilized word for *mount* but I told myself I was projecting. For all I knew this guy was married and in love and wanted to recruit me for commie points. But then he said, "You're the most beautiful communist I've ever met, Karina." And when he said my name, my heart felt it.

"Thank you, but you should check out the former Soviet Union—now they've got some babes—some real Natashas!" I said probably coyly.

"Okay. You're the most beautiful New York City communist—"

"American communist would have been fine," I laughed. "Anyway, I think of myself as a socialist. The ICP is probably my least favorite organization these days. I've never been a Stalinist but I was pro-Russia. The truth is, I've been feeling decidedly unrevolutionary these days."

Lenny T. came over and whispered something into his ear.

"They're relieving me. You want to find a quieter place?" he asked.

Nothing inside these organizations goes unnoticed; they try to control everything. I guess because they have so little control outside. I think they saw us talking and figured maybe they finally had me.

"Okay," I said. He led me downstairs through a labyrinth of dimly lit, beer-reeking rooms with low-hanging lamps and worn velvet sofas.

"Decidedly unrevolutionary? You *are* a challenge. Look, you know why they want you so badly—you're gorgeous! You are a beautiful girl. Look at you! They can rest their weary red brained, red eyes on you after thirty-two hours of ed board meetings. You've got to know they all want to do you," he ranted.

"Do me? They all wanna do me? . . .Well, it's a lovely sentiment, really. But for the commie record—nobody does me anymore. " I wasn't angry, I just had a point. I was actually glad he wasn't so P.C. that he felt he couldn't say something like that. In fact, the youthful, sexy, misogynist shit turned me on.

"I was being cute," he said.

"Still are," I said, thinking to myself, *What the hell are you doing? Go home to Sullivan and watch* Saturday Night Live!

"I think she likes me," he said. My face got hot, probably red. My awareness of my heated flesh paralyzed me. I was guilt-ridden. So I just sat there averting his gaze in my hot, red, enormous silence in the loudest damn warehouse. Yes, it was my turn for the half-clever repartee, but in my paralysis he might have offered a word, but he didn't. I think he was getting off on my agony. He knew what it meant. Then he put his very large and handsome hand on mine. We looked into one another's eyes for a good long time and then I stood up pretty abruptly and said, "I better go. Look, I live with someone. Things are not so good right now. This might make matters worse."

"Or better, darlin'," he said.

"Not unless you've got a place uptown I can stay in for a long time." I stretched out "long" to show him I was not making a serious proposition.

"Why uptown?" he asked.

"I work on 138th Street. I hate long commutes," I explained, still joking.

"How's 132nd and John Brown Boulevard?"

"I was kidding, Finn."

"I'm not. Come away and be my love and we shall . . ."

We laughed. And then we ended up talking for hours and not once about Ray Collins, the Middle East, unions, or the democrats. We talked about Hemingway, Pound, Lawrence and Joyce. Nietzsche, Schopenhauer and even Dan Dennett. We talked about souls. About evolution. We talked about that crazy website where you could download software to help you detect the tone of your e-mail—too many hot pepper icons and you might want to think twice about clicking "send." We talked about our families and about memes. And he asked to read my last story, "soft kill." I heard Sexton's *Candy* in the background.

Sullivan was wrong about that night: He'd be home before me. I guess it's because . . . I was *recruited*. And more than once. I called Sully the next morning to tell him I was okay. I lied and said I had stayed at a comrade's place downtown because it had gotten too late to come home. I told him I would be uptown in a few hours. I couldn't tell him over the phone that I was leaving him and without a paying roommate for his fabulous apartment! I would help him find someone, I told myself in the cab on the way there. Who was I kidding? Sullivan loved me. Or maybe now that I was leaving him he loved me. I guess he had always loved me. It hurt to watch this six-foot three-inch hunk of a man cry like a wounded child in a playground. I told him I'd be back for my stuff later and I left. The fact is, I knew he'd be all right. I probably would never have left had I not believed this.

I got back in a cab and rushed over to Finn's place with "soft kill" in my bag. The apartment was huge but it was in a blighted, mostly black section of the city—even the outer borders of it were far from gentrified. It was the kind of blight—severe, dangerous, without hope—that didn't attract hip, young, non-minority, liberal artists. It was more the kind of blight that attracted Irish communist spies. He was like a big piece of white rice in a bowl of black beans. And he seemed oblivious. The building itself had its share of loitering drug addicts and prostitutes and I guessed it was roach- and rat-infested but Finn swore it wasn't.

I rushed into his arms. He was big like Sully but somehow firmer and softer at the same time. I took in his smell, and we stared at each other kissing and giggling like school-children. We were happy. But what the hell were we doing? I knew this guy for less than twenty-four hours, left my boyfriend and my great river views. But despite not knowing him at all (I knew he was a communist so we shared certain basic values), when I looked into his eyes I felt like we had always known each other. I felt like I was having a déjà vu of a déjà vu of a déjà vu. And it was, corny and cliché as it is, as if the sparkle in his eye which lit up his entire face when he spoke was meant only for me. His smile stirred my heart wildly. But it was more than physical attraction—we somehow understood each other's cores.

We sat around talking for hours and he told me he wanted to read my story. We sat there on the couch as he read "soft kill." I felt silly sitting there with him, watching his reaction. But then he'd reassure me by caressing my arm or leg, or by looking up at me and just smiling. He loved the story. He loved the memes. He could go on and on about ideas, mercurially, just like me. And he could make love all night long—making me feel his love—just like me.

But all this cliché knowingness basically ended one perfect August day. We had been together for two months and I had never been happier. We had met for dinner near Columbia and decided to stroll around on campus. We sat on the steps. I remember catching a glimpse of another couple embracing and wondered if they were feeling like we did. And then I realized that not only did I not know how they felt, I couldn't know how Finn felt either. I pushed the philosophical question—the question of "other minds"— away, admonished myself and got back to loving him.

The air was dry and warm with a soft briny, fishy breeze

from the Hudson every so often that pushed his wavy light brown hair from his beautiful Irish features. It was probably a bad place to be kissing (even if it wasn't much) seeing as Sullivan was likely to be teaching a summer course or taking a seminar, but we were fairly unaware of the rest of the world. It seemed as the days went on, we focused less and less on the world. As it happened, it wasn't Sullivan who spotted us and ruined our perfect August day; it was a guy named Joe.

"Hey," he said.

"Joe, how you doing?" Finn seemed nervous and uncomfortable.

"Hey man, I'm good. Look, can I borrow your date for a few minutes?" Joe asked me in a goofy-confident, slick way.

I gave him the sure, go-ahead, we-can-suck-face-another-time gesture. And then Finn said, "I'm sorry, my beauty, I'll be a few minutes." I couldn't imagine who Joe was to Finn. He seemed so horrible.

I was so uneasy when he got back that I didn't even hear him say, "C'mon—I'll explain at La Carmelita's," until we were in a cab, and I replayed the events and dialogue in my mind as we rode in virtual silence down to 109th. We sat in the back of the restaurant next to a huge table of students. We hadn't uttered a word until Rosa came over and we said, practically in unison, *"Dos con leches, por favor."* Finn said, *"Y dos Tecatas, tambien."* Rosa gave him a funny look and I smiled at her—coffee and beer was not our usual.

"What's going on, Finn? Who's the guy?" Finn faced the entrance to the back room and he seemed to be keeping a watchful eye that way; he didn't answer me.

"You're starting to freak me out, Finn. What's going on?" I was trying to be calm but I was clearly agitated. Finn had expressions on his face I had never seen. Perhaps they were new to his physiognomy, too.

"Karina, Karina. I'm going to tell you who that guy is on condition you listen to the whole story, okay?"

"Yeah, okay. Who is he?" I was ready for anything—

"He works for the CIA."

—Except *that*.

"He's an agent—a secret agent. Not a big one, though—a little one," he confessed.

"Yeah? . . . What are you doing talking to an undercover CIA agent—even a little one?"

"I know this will sound—it's hard to believe—I'm not really in the ICP. I'm in SPA. I was recruited from a very small left-wing group in Dublin."

"SPA? I've never heard of it. What do you mean you're not in the ICP?"

"It stands for Socialist Peoples of America. I guess you could say we're a fairly new reformist organization—to the left of the social dems—which hopes to bring the left together."

"Hey, great, *wonderful!* So why the fuck were you talking to Joe the little secret agent?" I was really more curious than angry but felt I needed to be harsh, to show my anti-right sentiment—to question his soft left politics and to show him I wasn't trusting him. It was who I was—or who I was supposed to be—but I think for the first time in my life I was loving a man more than the idea of changing the world, more than loving abstract humanity. The image of his group, SPA—the proletariat taking the waters—was in my head, too, and it made me want to laugh. It was hard being angry.

"Karina, I'm a mole. That is, I'm a double mole. SPA sent me in to spy on the CIA. And ironically, perfectly, like one of your stories, the CIA sent me in to spy on the ICP. It's really quite unbelievable and I've never been sure I'd make it. But it's been easier than you would imagine. It keeps the ICP fairly safe, although there may be other moles I don't know about. And it's hell getting any information out of 'Intelligence.' They're maddening blokes, the whole lot of them. But anyway, one of the rules with these bastards is that I'm not supposed to get involved with a member."

"But I'm not a member. You know I don't belong to *any* organization, Finn," I said earnestly.

"Believe it or not, and this is going to upset you, beauty, and I'm sorry, Joe knows who you are."

"What do you mean he knows who I am?"

"These gits take pictures at all the left-wing demonstrations; they read the left's papers and do a lot of nasty surveillance crap. Believe me, beauty, you're a hard one to forget. Whether you're in or out is not the point for them—you're on the left and they don't want me with you."

"This sounds really dangerous. I mean, could they send you to prison for this?"

"For being a double secret agent against the United States government? Let's put it this way, if they can try to get a president of the United States out of office for getting his dick sucked, you can be very sure, my love, that they'll have my arse on a plate if they find this out."

"But kissing me on the steps of Columbia doesn't implicate you in any way or give you away, what's the problem? Anyway, it doesn't even mean we're involved. Just tell him it was nothing."

"You're right, my love. Kissing you, kissing you out in public, let alone at that damn university—it's full of all sorts of agents—does not say I'm a double mole. But being so damn ass stupid—really stupid . . . Look, it's against the agency's rules. They won't suspend me but it'll make them suspicious of my integrity—which is not a good thing. They're going to watch me. They're gonna listen. It's not good."

Finn told me that he did tell Joe it was a one-time thing, that we weren't involved. But he also said that Joe was going to report the kissing incident immediately and that he didn't want me to come back with him that night, said that they'd be watching from then on. He thought if we stopped seeing each other for a while they'd eventually stop monitoring.

Though Finn had become the thread which had started to close up my hole, my wound, of missing Sam and every other pain I ever felt, right then I felt the snag, and the stitches began unraveling. I felt alone. Vulnerable. I felt pins and needles down my arms and legs and on my chest.

I never realized how few single friends I had until I needed a place to stay. I couldn't hide out with a couple— too interruptive—and no room. So I asked Harry Schafsma to put me up. He was single and sweet on me, too.

Having to stay at Harry's was difficult. I wasn't twenty anymore. The move to Finn's was a quick and monumental life change for me—having to leave there after two months with no notice and hardly any of my things was hellish. I like my things. Most leftists like things. It's one of those contradictions you live with. Or at least it's a seeming contradiction. Most people who aren't on the left tend to think of communists as hippies who disdain material things—a sort of eastern/spiritual Buddhist thing. But real leftists *like* things—we have capital desires. We just want other people to have things too, regardless of their race and neighborhood. If Rosa Luxumberg were alive today, she'd like my Roseville vases, my Log Cabin quilt, my early twentieth-century Soviet Constructivist posters—why not?

I missed my sea glass and shells, too. And the pictures of my family. I liked having their photos around, though it took a long time to look at the picture of Sam. I had it up but would look right through it, not seeing it. It was only at Finn's that I had begun to finally see it.

So Finn brought a large bagful of clothes, makeup, notebooks, mail and a few books to La Carmelita's in the morning. He also brought my quilt. He had remembered what I told him about quilts with black—how they were hung in safe houses—places of refuge. He gave the bag to Rosa and I picked it up in the evening. The theory being that wherever he went someone was trailing him. They weren't trailing him enough so that they cared that he gave a big bag to Rosa and then watched Finn *and* Rosa all day long. At least Finn didn't think so. He wasn't a major player. He wasn't a threat to anyone. They just thought he was an agent who was fooling around with reds and it made them uncomfortable. For one, they had lost some valuable moles to the left. For another, it was the principle: if he couldn't obey that rule what else was he not obeying? But it wasn't heavy trailing. He was still working for them. They knew where he was and with whom he was spending his time (for the most part), and they knew he wasn't with me.

Finn brought my jeans, my Agnes B. tweed jacket, my Isabel Ardee suit, some blouses, some panties and bras, and my favorite tee-shirt to sleep in but that was it—and my cosmetics bag with my MAC mauve lipstick which I like to wear at night, especially in the fall, which was coming up soon. How long I was going to stay with Harry I didn't know. The last thing I could think of however was being a good guest, preparing for my classes, and thinking about my fall wardrobe.

At least I was up in the country. Schafsma was a much

better choice I realize now than Paul the obsessive-compulsive (Upper East Side) or even Sue Barry the expulsive who lives practically on campus. Although it was far away from school and I hate commutes, it felt like a great hideout, and the coordinator of the English program helped me synchronize my schedule with Harry's. Harry (the non-neurotic) and I never talked about the abruptness of my move—I think he was just so glad to have me stay with him that he was respectful of my privacy. He figured things hadn't worked with Finn and in a way they hadn't. I knew if I told anyone what I had done (leave Sully for a stranger and go into hiding for a man I'd known for two months) they would've called me a jerk and gotten me help. I guess that's why I didn't tell anyone.

I was feeling a bit hazy, sick, blurry and puffy. A layer of ragweed pollen, confusion, and the pining blues stuck to me like a thick layer of skin. But then Harry turned me on to the water holes. For the first few weeks before school, I probably went every day. As soon as I dove into that icy cold spring water it was as if I had molted, emerged from my daily cocoon. Having never been baptized, I performed this ritual with a new understanding of its power and a deep respect for damn cold water. I came alive. I was born and reborn again. It felt religious or spiritual—I wanted to shout Yawhzeh! I probably had a strange grin on my face like some crazy born-again Christian.

I'm not sure but I think the water saved me. It's like it was keeping the threads of my wounds from unraveling any further like cohesion tension. Or maybe it just reminded me of the Saint Lawrence.

Finn had my number at Harry's but had never called, and, of course, I was never to call him. There was no real reason he didn't call, I suppose. He could have easily called from a pay phone. They weren't going to bug *that*. They may not have even bugged his place. But he didn't call. He had gotten me to a place in my body, a very sexy ecstatic place, and then was gone. I missed him terribly—his body, his smell, his voice, his touch.

I needed him to sew me back together.

I went back and forth thinking something had happened to him, like he was arrested—or almost worse, thinking he decided he wasn't interested in me anymore, reconciled with an old lover . . . and in my very worst paranoid imaginings, thinking it was an elaborate scam to get rid of me and not have to tell me the truth—that he fell out of love. A psychotic coward. Harry kept me in good cheer, though. The ancient Greek women had quilts to keep them busy and faithful when their men were at battle; I had Harry and my writing.

And then one day he called. It was October already and I had almost said yes to a date with a very handsome restaurant owner—a four-star one. (It was just dinner, I should have gone but I turned him down, holding a flame for Finn.) He told me the unbelievable. He was a nasty mole. Not a double mole. A single mole. An Intelligence agent.

He told me that his love for me made him get out of spying on the ICP. He didn't want to hurt me, he said. But he couldn't abandon his work. He said he understood if I was not the least bit interested in him anymore and that he loved me despite our political differences. I told him I didn't understand how, but somewhere inside I did. He told me that my things were at his place and that he had paid for a few months if I wanted to keep my stuff there. He told me he was going to leave the country.

I asked him where he was going but he wouldn't tell me. Even though I could tell he wanted it to be over, he was also telling me he loved me. I was confused. I was angry he had lied to me and I was angry he was a damn spy against the left! How could I have misjudged someone so precisely? How could someone dissemble so well that you actually fall in love with ideas and values that aren't their own? But *was* that what I fell in love with, I wondered. There was more than just his values that drew me to him— something stronger and deeper—and it didn't make sense to me. The materialist side of me couldn't understand the conflict: he's a damn right-wing secret agent. What's to love? My idealist side screamed: Everything. And nothing. It's not what he is but who he is. Or is it not *who* but *what?* It was something essential. Anyway, I let him go. What could I do?

⌒

A few years later I was in the bay area for a conference on Freire. I saw two men leafleting at Berkeley for a paper called *United Socialists.* We talked and I found out the paper was the outfit of SPA. SPA? After Finn's admission I figured SPA was a fiction. I never once heard of them while I was in the city. It turned out there was a group in New York, but it was tiny. They had more support—larger "tendencies"—in California, Atlanta, and Detroit.

I was intrigued. Bill, the young handsome one hammered out the line like a good telemarketer:

"We're reformists, plain and simple. And we're Internationalists in the final analysis. We wanna bring the left together in this country . . . and ultimately worldwide. Marxism, historical materialism—they're not hard sciences—though many on the left still think so. Marxism is soft science and archaic. It's like being a strict Freudian without anything else. SPA is interested in modern socialism rooted in twenty-first century economics and power structure, not socialism based on the end of the nineteenth century.

"Things are different today. There's no hope to defend the gains of the Russian Revolution on a mass level ever again. What is the left—meager as it is in this country— thinking? We want to work within the system, primarily through changing legislation to eventually socialize the country—you know, like much of Europe. Without revolution. Europe's doing great things. Look at Germany, it just keeps going to the left. In the next ten years they'll be great and without a Bolshevik revolution, without bloodshed."

"At least you're not pretending *not* to be a reformist," I said, but he wasn't listening or didn't get it.

"Do you have kids?"

"No, I don't."

"Well, in many parts of Europe, for example, they give you a year of maternity leave with full pay, and you have the option to take off the second without pay . . . Yes, it's easier to do with homogenous groups . . . but that shouldn't stop us! The rest of the left calls us utopian when they're being generous."

Despite Bill's annoying sermon, I had to go to one of their meetings. It was in the hallway at their office that I saw Finn—from behind—walk into another office. He didn't see me. My heart raced, pounded, went into my stomach. My brain whirled.

I walked into the office where I had seen Finn disappear. It was fluorescently lit, smelled like ink, coffee and paper and was very quiet. I turned a corner and saw Finn, alone at a desk.

"Finn?" I said softly.

"Karina! Karina!" He stood up and held his arms open wide.

I didn't go closer and said, "Are you spying on them, too?"

"No. I'm not, Karina. I'm actually a true card-carrying member . . . I really was a mole for SPA. They pulled the plug on my New York operation. They got a tip the Feds were on to me. It was a mess. SPA wanted me out of the country for a few years. I've been home in Dublin, missing you."

"Why didn't you tell me?"

"I couldn't. I didn't want you to give up your life for me. Didn't want you to risk possible imprisonment which is what—didn't want you to have to decide to come into hiding with me or stay in New York."

"What life!? I did give it up for you! I left Sully and a great apartment for you—and I did it in one day—and I went into hiding in High Falls, and was prepared to do it for as long as you wanted! Yes, I like teaching. But who were you to decide for me? You thought you were sparing me? Or were you afraid I would have chosen to stay and you wanted to believe that maybe I would have come with you? Well you would have been right. I would have come with you, you fuck! I loved you. I really loved you . . . I still do. I even did when you were a damn secret agent for the damn CIA!" He was hugging me now.

Finn and I were burnt out. We lay in bed for days on end making love, eating, talking. Sex had always been so good with him—perfectly ergonomic, sensual and open. Now it was even better. It was so loving, I cried and laughed and came, all at the same time. I had never been happier in my life—cocooning and forgetting the world with the most perfect man. A man who made me softer, not harder, who filled up my holes. A man who could withstand my intensity and thrive on it, and who cared about the world as mightily as I did.

It might have been on the fourth day that Finn and I came to some important decisions. The world was not going to be saved, no matter how fiercely we cared or fought. Certainly we couldn't do it. We were feeling old and tired. We had talked about Onondaga, about how I probably had relatives at the reservation. We both knew where we wanted to go.

And that's where I am writing now, dear Sarah, as I smell the sweetness of black locust blossoms on this fiercely hot day, as I watch Wanni splash in the water. Watching her, it makes me think about all the passionate and strong women who came before her. Wanni's great-great-grand-mother, Frances, was born here, and the stories of her mother's fiery soul which have been told to me now, I tell Wanni, even though she is too young to understand.

I imagine this family is destined to go back and forth, recreating loss and new life. I have been told many stories but no one has offered a definitive explanation of why my family was kidnapped, stolen away. But I *am* starting to understand why Sylvia gave her child away to her sister. She was trying to mend the wounds that were still there with her white family, to create balance, harmony and a link. She gave her white family Indian blood. To strengthen it maybe? *To remind them.* It was an enormous sacrifice to make for trying to right the wrongs of others. I only under-stand sacrifice in some watered-down version. I spent some twenty years fighting against oppression—some times harder than other times, or trying to, in my various ways. But I see this is how I do it. I work and fight hard, pushing against obstacles until I'm spent; then I retreat to gain strength again.

Everyone here on the reservation gives me strength—a

feeling of optimism that I was starting to lose. This is the kind of living I've been longing for—it's unself-conscious, pure. Perhaps it's motherhood or communal living or a different stage of life. Maybe it's Finn who continues to keep my brain feeling alive and my heart open.

There is so much to teach Wanni, I realize, explicitly and implicitly, that I sometimes feel overwhelmed. She is the will of so many before her. She will learn the ways of this decent culture, but she will leave this place and perhaps struggle to understand or fit outside it.

Lately, I've been telling her about her father and me, and about something she should never run away from, never bury.

I tell her she was born from love.

# SIREN'S SONG

The minute I heard my first love story
I started looking for you, not knowing
how blind that was.
Lovers don't finally meet somewhere.
They're in each other all along.

*—Rumi*

Does writing in pleasure guarantee—guarantee me, the
writer—my reader's pleasure? Not at all. I must seek out this
reader (must "cruise" him) without knowing where he is. A
site of bliss is then created. It is not the reader's "person" that
is necessary to me, it is this site: the possibility of a dialectics
of desire, of an unpredictability of bliss: the bets are not
placed, there can still be a game.     *—Roland Barthes*

Culture is a byproduct of sexual competition for mates, where
individuals advertise their fitness by displaying their desirable
phenotypes (genius, creativity, taste).

*—Satoshi Kanazawa*

That was the story she gave him.

And it was pretty much the beginning of their story, too.

But before you read it, there's some things you should know, but that you might not understand. It's mostly because of the language. We do the same thing with our children. We tell them things they can't understand, but somewhere, in maybe a deep part, they do. And certainly, eventually they do. Language is strange like that. A word's meaning deepens with experience. Memes do, too.

There's this need to rush you. For you to understand. For it all to be known. Sorry. Just know, in the end, it will all make sense.

When she gave Caleb "Love Stories," it was the beginning of living them out. Maybe it would be "soft kill," or "Red Love," or maybe some other story. There weren't too many ways to go. Would he be Erich? Would it be a hot, quick affair where she would return to the warm love of her husband? Or would he be Finn? Her soul mate. The man she'd been waiting for. The man she would love unconditionally, eternally? Whoever he was going to be, he was there. He was there for her, to give her her story.

She told him "Love Stories" wasn't finished. She didn't mean there was another story to attach. Another chapter. She just meant it needed some revision. At least that's what she thought. Ah, but Caleb. He was an artist. He practiced the art of seeing the door or wormhole. And he knew how to get through, what to do.

If only she had known from the beginning how painful it would be in the end . . . *but perhaps that had been its strength. Not knowing.* Because it wasn't a story she could read or write with an ending stuck on as clear and eternal as black and white. No, their story had been real. And she had made a choice. *A choice to risk having loved and lost rather than having never loved at all.* Did she love? That's perhaps the biggest question.

"Love Stories" was his "shock point," his calling . . . he would be her "conscious shock." Like every process, there would be completion. The story *would* be finished; there would be an end.

Before there was speech, there was music;
before the orator, the artist of the song.
Language has its origins in art,
evoking feelings of feeling-part-of-something-larger-than-the-
self.                                   —*The Serpent Foundation*


Orpheus said to himself,
With my song,
I will charm Demeter's daughter;
I will charm the Lord of the Dead.
Moving their hearts with my melody,
I will bear her away from Hades.
                                   —*Homer*


Is it you, my prince? You have been a long time coming.
                                   —*The Sleeping Beauty*


Caleb reread the last line, *I tell her she was born from love*, and placed "Love Stories" inside a large wooden box which sat on his desk. His body felt strong, his heart open. He looked around for his CD.

Like all art, it was a seduction. Before she knew him she had written it for him. For one man. It was evolutionary. Female. Possibly spiritual. It was the *cultural display hypothesis,* la feminine. And she would understand it, though later, because she understood evolutionary psychology. She understood the theory that art is displayed and exhibited, particularly by males, as a strategy for broadcasting courtship displays to as many females as possible. It was consistent with *shift theory*, an interesting speculation she found on the Internet which said that roughly fifty-thousand years ago, those males who were particularly skilled at evoking through song and dance a feeling of *feeling-part-of-something-larger-than-the-self* were selected for by females.

But she was a woman. Her mating strategy was not about the many. It was about the one, the particular, the sublime. Her father, a brilliant and hard-headed filmmaker, told her art was to be shared, that without an audience, it wasn't art. She betrayed him. She betrayed art. She lacked even the faintest fraternal, androgenic urge to broadcast. It felt natural to her, to hide her paintings in the attic, and to keep her story, "Love Stories," the only one she'd ever written, concealed as a tiny icon on her computer. Imperceptible . . . yet certain. Even academically, her few published articles were the result of mandates from her department, not of her will. It wasn't her aim for "Love Stories" to be disseminated. She wrote it for herself.

And though she hadn't known it at the time, she wrote it for Caleb.

Her unconscious had the fairy tale worked out: the prince, once he sees the fair maiden locked in the tower (that is, reads her story), falls in love. He is her rescuer, her perfect fit. He understands, he appreciates and he knows how to save her— with the strength of her own feminine sexuality. *Rapunzel, Rapunzel, let down your hair . . .*

"Love Stories" was parts of her in fiction form crying— for help, understanding—for love. And because it represented her, the man who loved it and responded to her signal would be her complement, her beloved. Perhaps the strength of his anima could see through the phonemes, penetrate her core. It wasn't great fiction, certainly. And it wasn't her essence. But it had something. It was young, romantic, hopeful. And the man who responded—*where on earth was such a man?*—with appreciation, feelings, heat—he was her man.

But she was unaware of this plan—only glimpsing hints of it as it filtered from her unconscious to her preconscious, and there, from the gray matter shadows where her plan mostly loomed it would flash into conscious awareness, illuminating her will-to-live. Anyway, since she wasn't publishing "Love Stories," who was going to read it? Her husband liked it fine. Said it was well written in parts. Maybe it was too close.

Caleb.

Why did his name still excite her? Why did she want to hear it every day, still, now that the affair was over and she was supposedly onto other things? Even when she talked to her husband about him, it wasn't anything substantive—nothing her husband could have gained by some insight into her. It was about hearing his name. Caleb. "Was Caleb at the parent meeting?" "Caleb thought I should take that wall out in the kitchen."

Caleb.

Dendrites grew, neurons fired, hormones and pheromones flowed.

"This is Caleb," she said, months after the affair, in the dead of winter. (It wasn't to identify him; her husband had seen him before. It was to invoke his name. To bring Caleb back with utterance.) She pointed to a blurry picture inside a CD jewel case in a beautiful art and music shop in the small upstate town where they lived. It was hard to avoid it. It was displayed on a farm table in the middle of the store with a few other CDs and books. A fanciful sign on the table read "Local Artists." Lily, Caleb's daughter, stared at her from its cover in black and white—the perfect wood sprite. It was called *Lunaphile*. And she hadn't known about it. It was produced that year, she could see by the copyright, he just never mentioned it. She read, on a small card beneath the stack of CDs:

> Caleb Matthews's [Blind Rot, Earth As It Is, eros] and Drew Edwards's [eros] acoustics to the poetry of the Sufi mystic, Hallaj, will blow listeners' minds to the moon and beyond. . . . Matthews's mellifluous and erotic voice transforms Hallaj's prose into the sensual yet unearthly."—Daniel Gershon, *Lute and Lyre Magazine*.

She had understood Caleb's mating strategies. As quasi-alternative, small niche rock star, many years before they had met, he had broadcast to as many women as he could. (Though he never spoke about other women, she knew he had bedded enough to raise a village.) But he was a master teacher now, and a producer—a signal which meant a shift in his mating strategy. So, with this spiritual CD, she mused, he was back to broadcasting, though perhaps this time he was more particular, he was narrowing his audience, his eggs.

She felt strange discovering something new about him then. They were over. They weren't talking. She had none of his things (she even returned the shoelaces he had reluctantly given her out of the glove compartment of his beat up old truck which she had needed—it was only later she'd think they were probably Claudia's). Her only reminder of him that was tangible was a folded up piece of paper with *havtha@mindspring.com* written on it, which she left at the bottom of her purse. He had given that reluctantly too, knowing they'd be over soon, knowing it might mean trouble for him later. And she just felt strange, almost like she was violating some important principle of the cosmos, holding that square piece of plastic with his image on it, with Lily's, with his Orphic music, and his ambery, low-god voice. Though it was late, too late in fact, pieces of his puzzle and their puzzle were coming together finally—in her daydreams, when she awoke after a long sleep, in her songs.

Like discovering the CD, the ideas and realizations she stumbled onto, too. And sometimes they poured out. Fragments of conversations and scenes flooded her when she least expected them, attempting an accurate revision of the past. Childhood stories he had told her, which she had forgotten during the affair, insinuated themselves now, as if they were her memories, while she swept. And memories of subtle hesitations, incongruous gestures, perhaps lies, finally made sense. But why hadn't they been there when she needed them most, she wondered. She wrote them all down.

☞

At least she knew she was asleep.

Though her desire had burrowed underground, she had been able to find some amount of comfort in its dormancy, in the rest. And it had been good for her and the world, for a while, anyway, that she believed in her roles as mother, wife, teacher, artist—that all the things she did *mattered*. So she sang lullabies to her sexual, procreative impulses, without knowing, and was, for the most part, satisfied with her social productivity.

Her problem during this long sleep, in this warm place, this burrow, without sexual longing, was that she no longer recognized herself. And so her paintings were always about that, existence, essence . . . trying to find herself. Only her reason was lulled into believing there'd be no more desire.

Of course, she had had misery and bliss before. *Was the misery and bliss, in the end, about becoming comfortable?* she wondered. Were the struggles with men and the struggles with her husband all about reaching this calm?

These questions kept coming. From her lucid dream state,

this halfway somnambulate point between satiety and desire, slumber and wakefulness, being a person and being a woman (our sex and humanity don't always share strategies), she was beginning to feel a little uncomfortable, comfortable. Her friends certainly appeared happy with their families and careers, but the cultural veil was unable to hide her truth from her. She was unable to wrap herself within it, with her cohorts, safe from desire. And, of course, the longer she tried to wear this veil that shrouded everyone around her, the more transparent it became, and the more she realized she could not get under it. *What is the price of too much prohibition? . . . When the inner censor grows too strong, prohibits too much?*

But she was good. Or certainly trying to be. She wasn't *looking* for light. To be woken. She was only half-asleep though, and light travels fast.

It didn't help matters that she had read a strange, short piece in her college alumna magazine. That she read:

## My Other Story
### *by Calla Jones*

*Alice went timidly up to the door and knocked. . . . "There's no use in knocking," said the Footman. . . . "Please then," said Alice, "how am I to get in?" "Are you to get in at all?" said the Footman. "That's the first question, you know."*

I wasn't a bitter housewife. I was well cared for by my adoring, wealthy husband who cherished my skills at being a great mom, a great cook, the Martha Stewart of Westchester. I was just so unhappy in my marriage. And unhappy with my life. I felt suffocated and I felt like my husband was keeping me from fully living and creating.

We met at college. I was a cultural anthropology major, he, an English major. I thought he'd become a writer or editor; instead, he became an advertising executive. But that was the ride we were on. It was hard to complain with all that money coming in. I don't know why I didn't pursue my field. It was the late '70s, after all.

Well, I had so much desire in me, sometimes I felt like I was going to explode. I *wanted* the men at those dinner parties we'd go to. Especially the artists. They really got to me. I wanted to be near them, I wanted them in me, I wanted to be close to art. I felt so empty. Like there was no art in me. And every time some handsome artist asked me what I did, I just wanted to lie. To make up some story about how I was a sculptor or a filmmaker or a writer. But I couldn't, of course. And so, the conversations were always short. *Oh, you stay at home with your kid. That's one of the hardest jobs there is.* And then they'd be off.

Anyway, I was still young when I started seeing the door. I was maybe thirty-one. And I think it was the zeitgeist, all these women around me who were so liberated, that made me finally realize how simple it was to change my life. All I needed to do was slap that Footman at the door and say, "Who are you to ask me if I'm to get in? Outta my way!" And it was then that I started to see that there were other stories I could be living.

Finally, when I felt like I was going to burst, I signed up for a filmmaking course at the community college not far from where I lived. It's where I met my second husband, and it's how I became a filmmaker. . . .

We have many stories in us. We have to listen to our stories. When we feel there's no where to go, like we don't know where to go, like there's only one story in us, or none; that's when we must open our eyes. Wake up! The simplest observation, the simplest change, can open a new world. We mustn't feel paralyzed by our own censors—by our own crazy-frog-footmen. There are so many stories inside us we can live. The trick is knowing which story you want and having enough courage to live it.

We women are all artists in some way or another. It's about accepting ourselves as artists. Artists with desire. We're sexual *and* social. We can reproduce not only flesh and blood but artistically: images, ideas, music. You mustn't bury your desire. Do not bury the art within you. Sing and dance, paint, sculpt, act, draw, edit, film, photograph, write, direct, montage, create, build, design. And love.

It began in September. Julian had been talking about his friend Lily for weeks.

"Mom, Lily and I got married today." "Mom, Lily is my best friend." "Mom, do you know what Lily is short for? Lilibel." When she'd pick Julian up from school she'd have a chance to spend time with Lily, and she felt drawn to her, just like Julian. Lily had a puppy dog quality and something more—a hunger which stimulated her own oxytocin-addicted body. She wanted to take care of Lily, to mother her. She felt like she had always known her.

On a morning after having given Julian a kiss goodbye, she closed the classroom door behind her and found Lily standing in front of her, wanting to get in, holding the hand of a beautiful man. She had been bringing Julian to that artsy private school for five years, since he was three, and she had never once seen a man like this there, in fact, around anywhere. It's hard to know what exactly made it all happen. Was it Caleb alone who was able to pull her out of that dark place? Or was it just that she was ready and he was there, that old saying about *when the student is ready, the teacher appears.* It was probably both.

"So you're Lily's dad," she said almost ecstatically.

"That's right." He bent down to hug Lily. "Have a good day, sweetie. Your Mom's picking you up today. Okay?"

"Okay, Dad. Bye," Lily waved at them both.

They walked out of the school together as she explained how Julian had been talking about Lily almost obsessively. Caleb admitted he had heard about Julian. But they could have been talking about anything. It wasn't about signified, or meaning. It was the signified of signifier. It was sensual. How the sounds sounded. And how the eyes lit. How their bodies warmed. It was here, in this moment, that they both saw their fates together. How they each responded to their singular vision was another matter.

Ordinarily, because she was married, she would have been distant with Caleb, possibly avoiding him. She did this with attractive men. (It always seemed to her that less attractive men understood her friendliness.) However, in those days she had felt optimistic and vibrant and had decided to stop thinking and worrying, and to just be. To feel free and alive and let her hair down. To bring happiness to the world. To be egalitarian in her friendliness. Talking to a beautiful man should not lead to his bed, she assured herself. Caleb was beautiful, certainly, but they were parents, married, it was safe.

Maybe one fear she had was that her eyes and her flushed skin would give her away. He must have thought so. His take on this event, she found out later, was that he thought she was signaling to him, that she was interested in him. Later she would discover that he came by this strategy naturally—it was evolved. In her research she found that most men will assume that when a woman is friendly she is receptive to sex and behave accordingly. This is because men are the direct descendants of other men who shared this cognitive strategy, this algorithm, or brain module. Men who didn't assume a friendly woman was interested in sex left less genes. The survival of the *friendly equals she's interested* gene. So Caleb was programmed to see this. And she? She had probably been programmed by evolution to be sensitive and discriminating. Women who signaled often or inappropriately, or indiscriminately, may have gotten raped, killed, or stuck with "inferior" genes to pass on. Added to this was her guilt. She was programmed by "culture" to be "good." She was married. She feared the pull.

Think of him as a mom, she told herself. He's a *mom*. But it was her determination not to view Caleb as a "man" which backfired for her. Because it made her light, carefree and attractive—and it made her available. In the end nature won out—it was stronger; it helped deceive her to free her of the cultural and personal constraint. Had she been aware of it, it would not have worked. Mother Nature helped her fool herself; *Maternatura* had less admirable plans.

When she saw Caleb again at the school, her body smiled and heated. It felt like it did when she went into the sun during her period to be soothed by its radiance, only better. He was the sun. He was the first man in years whose very presence alone woke her slumbering body. She held the gate to the school open for him and tried to repress her feelings. She wished she were more beautiful. She felt drained and tired and feared it showed on her face.

Inside, they said goodbye to their kids, but Caleb seemed to want to chat, there, in the hallway. Had she been young and single she would have left, waiting for that perfect moment when the goddess of sleep and health had bestowed her magic upon her in his presence. But she was not young and single, and to wait for the aesthetic gift—it could be weeks—was pointless. So, to keep herself from fleeing and sweating she reminded herself, *he's a mom.* Still, he made her nervous. He stood there holding her with his gaze, not speaking. Until finally, in an attempt to shield herself from his glare she said, "Julian wants me to stay today and go to the farm with them."

"Are you able to do that?" he said.

"Well, I could cancel a couple of appointments. . . ."

"Yeah? What do you do?"

"Well, I'm an adjunct . . . But I'm renovating my house—that's what my appointments are for."

"What do you teach?"

"Philosophy."

His eyes lit up. She tried not to notice.

"So I'm wondering if I should cancel my appointments. I'm so tired. And hungry. I don't think I can make it to the farm. . . ."

"Why are you tired?"

It was a simple question, but it seemed so bold, so presumptuous. It was her move. She could have given him a cursory answer, the way most people would have done in a situation where a virtual stranger asks a personal question. But that wasn't like her.

"Um, well, it started a few months ago when Julian was sick, and he'd get me up like four times a night. It's such a shock to be woken from your sleep. There are people who can handle their REM being interrupted, but it makes me psychotic. My psyche craves completion. . . . I needed my dreams to have endings. Anyway, after he was better, I'd still keep getting up—in the middle of my dreams, like a habit. And my dream life was really affected. . . . You know?"

"I do."

"I was insane for a while. It was like my right hemisphere was trying to, I don't know, work the shit out the next day. Kinda like dreaming while you're awake. And I began to have the sense I'd feel better not sleeping at all. It's like food—if you're very hungry, sometimes it's better not to eat at all than to have just one grape. And now, I finish my dreams but I wake up at about four in the morning and write until Julian gets up."

"What do you write?"

"I write my dreams. My four-in-the-morning dreams. I write until about seven . . . I don't really write my dreams . . . I'm being poetic. I've been working on this story—it's actually two stories—which I'm constantly revising and rewriting. So that's why I'm tired. But I'm not crazy anymore. Well, maybe a little."

He loved that she talked to him this way. He loved that she talked like that. He loved her sweet voice.

"I like the word you used to describe your waking. *Shock.*"

It was starting to get weird. She was starting to feel dizzy. And it wasn't just the lack of the Appolinian—all those dream-images she never saw from four to seven in the morning, that made her weak and hot and a little bit crazy; it was also Caleb, feeding her hungriest receptor sites—pulling her toward a dopamine rush she both feared and craved. And the beginnings of a flu.

"And hungry?" he asked.

She was sweating slightly. She hoped he would stop drilling her. She had already said too much. She always said too much. There was this desire to be known. And every time she talked too much, she scolded herself: *learn from this discomfort. Do not give yourself away.*

But it really wasn't her saying too much, or what he was asking that made her sweat; it was how he was asking. With a serious intensity. Almost as if his life depended on her every answer.

"Maybe I'm not hungry, actually, I'm just . . . I'm . . . I think I *am* going to go to the farm," she said out of desperation and put her hand on the doorknob.

"Have a good time," he said.

"Bye," she said as she opened the door and walked into the classroom with the other good parents, feeling sick.

It took her more than two weeks to recover. Throughout it Julian had asked for Lily incessantly. And in that time she would often stare at the separate phone numbers listed in the school directory for Caleb and Kate Matthews. Two numbers tied by one name. She worked hard during her sickness, as if working a mathematical theorem, an algorithm, to add those sets of numbers together. Seven and seven is one. One and one equals one. The possible scenarios. *Maybe the number next to his name is his office, the number by her name, the family's.* But why was she thinking about this? What did it matter? The alternative, the obvious, that Caleb and Kate weren't together, that those numbers represented distinct homes, separate lives, she forced out of her skull, as simply as she forced Forsythia branches.

Now that she was better she could navigate the world of play dates. She got out the directory and called the number listed for Kate, though she had never met her. It felt inappropriate to call Caleb. She was afraid to call him. She was afraid of what that deep part of her saw as an inevitability—and she wasn't ready. Anyway, that murky part figured, if they were to be together, or if they were "meant" to be together, in the end, then calling Kate wouldn't change it. So, as usual, she would go out of her way to avoid him. It was better, sans guilt.

When she called Kate, she got an electronic voice message. She hated those things—she never knew if she had dialed the right number. So, for Julian, or because she took the machine as a sign, or both, she called the other number.

"Hi, Caleb, this is Julian's mom," she said, nameless, as if her identity were insignificant.

"Hi," he said.

"I'm calling for a play date with Lily. I tried the other number but got an electronic voice and I wasn't sure if it was the right number. That's why I've called this number," she explained.

"I'm glad you called. I like human voices too," he said.

They planned the play date for the next day when she would pick the children up from school and take them to her home. In the years of play dates this was the first that had ever been planned for the next day—she made a note of that. And then he told her that he and Kate were divorced.

This seemed harder to force out. She heard the words. The trick was to lock them somewhere in the gray matter where they could not find reason. To jumble the sounds and morphemes. To forget. But the struggle just made it worse. In resisting the meaning of the words, she heard him, his voice.

What she heard was a certain self-consciousness, something she recognized in herself. And in the quality, the timbre and tone of it, was an ancient language—song-like—which spoke to her primordial nature. It said, *I want to devolve into you. To disappear and appear. I want to fuck you and make love to you until we dissolve all boundaries. I want you to choose me. And you will.*

"I'll see you tomorrow," he said.

"All right," she said.

"Bye," he said.

"Bye."

She gripped the phone tightly as she set it down, as if this could prevent his pull.

That morning on her way back home from dropping off Julian she saw Caleb walking to his car. They said hello, mentioned the play date and kept walking. Then he started walking back toward her.

"What's up?" she asked, putting her hair back with a barrette.

"My car's blocked in."

She wondered, *why'd he come over to tell* me? But instead said, "What are you gonna do?"

"Walk you home." Androstenone perfumed the air.

This seemed like such a come-on to her that to prevent herself from sweating, she convinced herself he was merely wanting to see the kind of a home Lily would be playing at. She thought to refuse his bold gesture, which is what she wanted to do, would be taken badly, would make things unfriendly at the school. And she was afraid to lose him. She saw and felt the romance but couldn't face it. And so she repeated her mantra to herself: *He's a mom. He's a mom. He's a mom.*

She lived about half a mile from the school, and though it was cold, the sun was shining. They walked through an open field and past an old street with stone houses. Caleb wasn't a mom. He wasn't a regular dad. He was beautiful and he walked fast.

But she kept up with him.

They passed all the bullshit of talking about the kids, the school, weather, and town meetings and talked about philosophy and spirituality. He told her about the spiritual sage

Rajingiev. And about his production/recording company, Havtha. Though on paper he owned and ran Havtha, he explained, most of the profits went to Heliosen—the Rajingiev-inspired, esoteric, quasi-cultish, new age community where he lived and was a master teacher. Rajingiev and Heliosen were familiar to her but beyond seeing "Rajingiev" in new age bookstores she didn't know much else.

She told him about the triptych she was painting.

And he told her, "For the past two weeks I've been trying to get your number. Lily finally told me Julian's last name, but you weren't listed. And Lily's mom never told me there was a school directory. I just got one yesterday, and I was going to call you." This didn't sound like he was after a play date—at least not with Julian. She took a deep breath and lied to herself some more.

The front door was wide open when they got to the house. Her contractor was there finishing up his latest project. His eyebrows actually raised when he saw Caleb—he knew her husband. For hours and hours she and Caleb talked at the dining room table and then, later, the living room floor. He made her talk mostly and he listened. This felt so unnatural to her but finally she gave in. It felt like a karmic gift from the gods.

She told him about developmental philosophy (the class she taught, and how it dealt with the question of nature versus nurture, and epigenesis). And about her interest and research in evolutionary psychology—the new science of the mind. She also told him about aesthemiotics, and many of her baby theories—like her global theory of depression—that it serves as a mating isolation mechanism, or natural selection pressure and about why she thought PMS had evolved:

"It's a signal to human males to stay away, don't waste your time, invest time in females not 'displaying' low progesterone signals."

"What's a low progesterone signal?" he asked.

"Well, when the female body dips in progesterone, after mid-cycle, or in menopause, there's a lot of behavioral and physical 'symptoms.' Some women act angry, some break out—observable, fairly unattractive things. Men find women most attractive when they're ovulating."

"That's interesting. How is that? I thought the whole point was that ovulation is hidden," he said.

"Well, that's been the dominant theory for a while—that our concealed ovulation fostered pair-bonding, right? If you don't know when a woman is ovulating, you'll spend more time with her sexually and also mate-guarding. But they're showing that men may in fact know when a woman is ovulating by sensing her particular pheromones. When a woman is ovulating, a man will find her 'smell' more pleasurable than at any other time. There also appears to be an overall relative lightening of the skin, which, studies seem to show, men 'instinctively' find attractive."

He nodded.

She removed the barrette, which was holding some of her hair back, and held it in her hand. Auburn fell down around her face, and Caleb's eyes widened.

She hadn't been aware of herself letting it down, until Caleb's reaction—his change of focus. So, feeling somewhat self-conscious, she put it back up. (Naturally, the hair up-and-down routine excited him.)

"Anyway, I think PMS is also a time for a female to consider what she did 'wrong' or what she needs to do to get fertilized. I think that's why women often feel depressed, unattractive, and unworthy during PMS. My hunch is that pregnancy alleviates the negative symptoms. If you don't want to feel bad every month—get pregnant!" Caleb worked hard at listening to her. He could even repeat what she had said to him. It was part of his practice, his "work." And it was good, too, because otherwise he would have just watched her mouth. And her breasts. To put his head there and suck.

"I also think postpartum depression served an important function for our ancestors. . . . There are some female mammals who go into seclusion after giving birth, not moving for days, maybe months. I'm thinking in our early environment, millions of years ago—evolutionary psychologists call it the EEA (the environment of evolutionary adaptedness)—the 'depression' could have helped the mother focus on the needs of her baby, keeping her near and out of harm's way. Nowadays it's maladaptive because our living rooms are pretty safe."

Caleb felt a bit intimidated, but he succored his ego by telling himself that these questions of the material world mattered little. Why there was PMS was insignificant. Everything he cared about and thought about was beyond evolution. Still, he was impressed. And he could feel that she was spiritual in the layers below and he wanted to find that place, that source—for her as well as for him.

As the hours passed she opened and became more personal, less guarded: "It's hard for me to take in compliments. It's like I'm protecting myself from the pain of identifying with something. To accept a compliment is to give power to the other—to possibly hurt me later with criticism, or worse. And it is to identify myself with something, something I have created, or chosen, or had luck in being or obtaining. And it's like, 'You don't like my painting? . . . Well, it doesn't bother me, because I am not identified with it. I don't *own it*, I'm not *attached*.' And yet I know that's bullshit, somewhere. The worst part is I don't feel much. I'm numb most of the time. And I don't think it's by choice. Or maybe it is. Maybe it's from my eastern philosophy days—maybe this is non-attachment, 'wisdom,' 'clinging to the void.' All I know is it seems it's been thrust on me. As if painful experience leads to this. Suffering leads to this. Skin develops calluses for good reason. And if they're not needed, they disappear. The mind seems a lot slower to heal. It's more protective. I want to feel, but I prevent myself."

He was listening to all her crap so intently that she thought he was going to tell her time was up and he'd see her again next week for another session.

He said, "Maybe you don't take in compliments because you don't respect the opinions of the people who are giving you the compliments."

She thought about it for a moment. "You know, you may be right." And then she thought, *I already respect his.*

They drank tea. Whatever she was having, he had too. This was so unlike her experience with her woman friends who came over—either they resisted having anything or they always had a different kind of tea than the tea she was drinking. Even when she waxed poetic about a vanilla hazelnut Chai or decaf mint green tea, invariably, they'd want something else. This bothered her. When she went to a friend's house she drank what they drank or offered. Why were her women friends so contrary? Why did they feel the need to separate, to create boundaries, to retain power? Caleb was like her. Or at least he acted like her. Maybe more so.

He told her about his community, Heliosen. About their dictum "focus, take aim and commit to love." He explained some of the principles and ways of living that they followed. Among them, really listen to people. Don't interrupt people while they're talking. Don't break your word. Be what others want you to be. Be present. Awake. Pay attention. Self-observe: attend to your own physical sensations, posture, gestures, voice. Understand your "personality" to help find "essence." Concentrate on physical work. Rise at five. Meditate. And be useful, an instrument.

He talked about transcending to the sun where there were less "laws" and where a soul could be freer.

And about quantum physics, the Bohm-Einstein condensate experiment, the Isaiah scrolls, and parallel universes.

He said that at every moment there were probably many, many possibilities occurring simultaneously—parallel universes—and that each outcome lay in rest, as potential, until they were awakened by our choices—that reality was already created but that we chose our fate or reality by where we placed our focus, in the form of thought, feeling, emotion and prayer.

He said there was an art to it—being able to see the door or wormhole to a parallel universe—and knowing how to get there, what to do.

And that, at the practical level, in our earthly forms, it was about conscious, unautomatic reaction. How by observing one's habits and reactions one could eventually break free of them. How not to be bound by one's history, the patterns of our individual lives, or the patterns of our species. How not to get one's buttons pushed.

But she *wanted* her buttons pushed. The spiritual-science side of Heliosen was likable, she thought, but the rest sounded like good manners to her and a lot of it was about doing what she did naturally and which she had spent her whole life trying to get away from: being attentive and aware of everything, including oneself. Trying to give people want they want. Later, she would realize that Heliosen was helping this alpha male to become more feminine, or to awaken that aspect in him, as a survival mechanism, nothing more. And she also realized, as essentially hyper-feminine, that she had been working at becoming more masculine, also to survive. Each was working at balance within themselves. But here, on the floor, next to the fireplace, where they sat and talked and gazed into each other's eyes more seriously than she would have preferred, the answer seemed much more basic, pure, eternal. And they both saw it.

She brought him to her attic and showed him the triptych she was working on. It was in the Pre-Raphaelite style, but with a twentieth-century edge.

"It's Artemis, Athena and Aphrodite," she said.

"They look like you. . . . They're beautiful," he said.

It felt good and right showing it to him; she knew he understood.

Downstairs, they sat in her sunroom, slightly inebriated from the scent of her climbing jasmine, potted herbs of rosemary, sage and thyme, and a flowering orange tree. She got up to water the ficus. Caleb studied her.

"You have a grace about you. Do you dance?"

"Not anymore. I used to, though. I studied Graham and a little Isadora Duncan. . . ."

"Yeah, I thought so. You seem to have a gift of movement, but I also see there has been a practice—work. Do you miss it?"

"A little bit."

"You should come by Heliosen on Wednesday nights. We dance then. It's a very special kind of dance, based on specific movements in Rajingiev's system."

"Hmmm, sounds esoteric. I don't know . . ."

"Well, think about it. I think you'd like it."

"All right, I'll think about it."

"We also sing on those nights. Do you sing? You have a lovely voice . . . You *must* sing . . ." he said.

"Yeah, wow . . . you're good . . . I used to. In high school, in college, I was in a few bands," she said, walking into the kitchen to fill the watering can. Caleb walked through the door behind her.

"May I have one?" he asked.

"Of course, please," she said.

Caleb took an apple from a wooden bowl on the counter. He thought about wormholes. About hyperspace. About other universes. Other realities. Focus. Vision. He closed his eyes and prayed before he took a bite.

"That's how I'm going to see you. . . ."

"What do you mean?"

"Music. It's perfect. . . . Let me produce you . . . I'll play for you. And we'll get Drew—we used to play together—he's an incredible bassist . . . he's gonna really like you. . . . This is great—for a second there, I thought I was going to have to renovate your house to see you—"

He seemed to know exactly what he wanted and it was her. She was powerless. She felt like she did as a kid at the ocean when the waves would knock her down near the shore and carry her with them for what seemed an eternity, until she was close enough to shallow ground to surface.

"Renovate my house? You do construction, too?"

"I do. It's very much valued in the community. Simple, physical . . . most of the jobs we have, inside and outside of Heliosen, tend to be physical. It's related to being a good 'householder,' as Rajingiev calls it. It's about developing attention. Doing repetitive physical work provides an immediate object for attention. It's sort of the first foundation. Anyway, what I do at Havtha is a little lofty for them. It's definitely out of the ordinary. But it's needed. I've produced a lot of these spiritual CDs and Heliosen's done well from it. Anyway, I'm glad I don't have to paint your house to see you. I'm very glad it's music instead."

"But what if you don't like my voice?"

"I'm gonna like your voice. But if I didn't—which won't happen—it doesn't matter. It's a way for us to see each other. Okay?"

"Okay. But I care if you don't like my voice."

"I'm going to like your voice. I can tell by the way you talk, by the way you move. . . . Look, tomorrow I'll bring by some of my music, and soon, we can start playing together. All right? . . . It's going to be great!"

She went into the kitchen to get more water and he followed her.

As she filled the watering can, he said, "Before I go, there's something else."

"What is it?" she asked, putting the watering can on the counter.

She was now sitting on a radiator warming herself, and he was standing in the threshold to the kitchen. She wondered if he was turned on by the sight of her squirming around, adjusting the heat to different parts of her bottom, because he kept pausing for long stretches in the middle of what he was saying. She couldn't stop, though; the heat felt so good, but then it would get too hot and she'd have to move her ass around again. She thought he was going to kiss her.

"That story of yours—can I read it? I really would love to read it."

"Ah . . . um, I'm not sure where it is."

"Oh, come on, you know where it is."

"You're right, I know where it is, but . . . it's not finished."

"That's okay. C'mon, go get it," he said.

"You don't want to read it."

"I very much do want to read it. Please, let me read it, you have to let me read it. I won't leave here unless you give it to me."

She gave him "Love Stories." He wanted to love the siren. He knew he would. He took her art home and was seduced.

Later that day, before she picked Julian up from school, she had a sudden urge to rearrange her room (yes, it was her husband's room too, but it never felt like it), go through her closets, and clean. The greens there had been feeling oppressive, flat, somewhat nauseating. But she hadn't had the energy or vision until now. So she took away the green oil painting, the green vase, the green fabric draping on an antique dress form, and painted her sea-green bookshelf white. But she brought the green, green ficus from the sunroom and put it next to the window near the bed. She wanted it all white, but alive. And so after all the activity, she laid there on her white sheets, looking at the white wall and the violet cosmos from her garden in a glass vase on the white-painted bureau, the ficus, the maple tree outside her window, the sun coming in, and she was happy. He was reading her story. He was reading it.

The next day he showed up at her back door unexpectedly.

"Your story was very wonderful," he told her. They were standing on her back porch. "I've never really read anything like it. I liked Karina . . . liked the sexy parts. Thought the African quilt thing was cool . . . breaking patterns. Like how you think in threes: the birth, life, death 'baby theory'; the *reading, writing, and living* meme. I really liked that. You know, 'three is a magic number,'" he sort of sang.

"Yes it i—i—is . . ." she sang back, putting her foot up on the rail. He smiled at her, as he followed her foot up to the crease near her thigh.

"Oh, and there's a part . . . when Sarah feels air leaking from her chest . . ." he said.

"Yeah?" she said.

"Do you know that air is associated with the heart chakra?" he said.

"No, I didn't . . . but that's very interesting," she said.

"I'd really like to read more."

"I don't have any more . . . not fiction—but if you'd like, I've got a recent article in the *Journal of Developmental Philosophy*—on memes and cultural evolution . . ."

"I *would* like."

And then he gave her a CD.

"Eros?" she smiled.

"Yeah, it was my last band. Look, the last song is an instrumental, you should sing with it, it'll be good for you . . . I've got to go. . . . And by the way," he said, walking off her back porch, "your story's not the only thing that's wonderful. . . . Bye."

"Bye," she said.

Eros. She was fixated on it. The Greek god of carnal love, passion, erotica, libido, the will to live, *sore* spelled backwards.

Not surprisingly, she liked his music. It was alternative rock, but with an ethereal quality, and the chords reminded her of music she wrote on the piano.

His music also confirmed a belief she was developing, though reluctantly. A belief about outward appearances, about signs. That it was all right to trust what she saw. That there was a strong correlation between sign and signified, between the look of a thing and its meaning. And that the beauty of an object, at least, what was beautiful to her, often had intrinsic and functional value for her.

She had discovered it was that way with cars. When her husband bought himself a new Volkswagen Jetta, she didn't like its looks—the lines, the curves, the gray-blue color, nothing appealed. He told her it rode like a dream, so she drove it—almost off the road, it was that awkward to her.

Her 1974 sea-green convertible Triumph was love at first sight, though. And inside, driving, it felt right—its size, the heaviness and tightness of the steering wheel, the way she could feel the road.

It was reassuring to know that she could trust her ocular instincts and impressions. She didn't know how it worked, it just worked.

## sex energy

An inherited collective image of woman exists in a man's unconscious, with the help of which he apprehends the nature of woman.                        —*Jung*

But Orpheus had no rival . . . There was no limit to his power when he played and sang. No one and nothing could resist him.                                     —*Homer*

Caleb's aural seduction was in many ways the most exciting and erotic period of the affair for both of them. She would bring her cordless phone into the bathroom, turning the fan on so her husband couldn't hear. All he knew (and this is why Caleb was so clever) was that she was singing with him. He was pleased for her. He knew it was something she had enjoyed when she was younger, and he supported her effort.

"I'm hard all the time," Caleb told her. "I can't get my work done. All I do is think about you."

"I'm . . . I can't say," she said.

"C'mon, what?" he said.

"I can't. It's too . . . No." She felt vulnerable, embarrassed.

"What is it? Tell me."

"It's very difficult, I feel . . . no, I can't."

"Please tell me."

His persistence turned her on, but it frightened her, too. She gave in.

"Well, I'm wet a lot. I don't remember ever being this way. Does that sort of turn you off?" she asked.

"No, not exactly. It makes me want to come over is what it does."

"Well, you know that would be difficult right now," she said.

The challenge of the other male only made Caleb harder and his focus sharper. Their bodies became more beautiful as the days went on and they felt stronger, energized. They couldn't sleep and they hardly ate—they had never felt better.

Caleb had been working very hard at Havtha but had now lost his will to work. He wanted her. He believed in her. He'd drop by her house in the middle of the day and spend a few hours with her, talking, usually under a sugar maple in her yard.

Rajingiev's philosophy was complex, mathematical. When Caleb talked in this foreign language, and especially when he used math, she could sometimes fool herself he had access to a world beyond her. She was aroused by his deep understanding of the physics of music, of sacred geometry. Her chest would flush at certain simple things he'd say, like, "Everything has a shape, and every shape has a meaning." Her pubis would swell at "the beauty of a crystal is really a shadow version of a higher dimension—probably the tenth."

She also was impressed by the precepts Caleb lived by, like

"keep your word," and "don't interrupt." And though they weren't really different from the ones *she* lived by, his "work" made her that much more self-aware. So when they talked in these early days, she practiced not interrupting—a basic Rajingiev principle. It wasn't too hard. Her interrupting was an acquired habit, what Rajingiev would have called *personality*. Her "essence," in fact, could have listened to Caleb forever.

He told her about the law of the triad, also called the law of three: "Creation can only happen when there are three forces present: an active first force, a passive second force and a reconciling third force—a force which acts upon the other two.

"Think of the C major scale: there are points of 'missing semitones'—sharps and flats. The missing semitones between *mi* and *fa* and *ti* and *do* are shock points—where a process can go wrong, but where, if a new influence—a corrective or 'conscious shock'—a third force—is introduced, the intended impulse can reach completion."

"That's too abstract for me—" she said.

"Okay. The law of three works within us. It explains the forces of an event. Like in sex, a man is first force, that is, active; and a woman is second force—receptive. With sex energy, which is the reconciling force or third force, a new being can be created. The thing about these forces is that they aren't fixed. Third force in one event can become first force in another. That's Rajingiev's law of the octave. An ascending or evolutionary octave is one where a conscious shock is applied—one that is informed by knowledge, driven by effort, and results in understanding—where we come to stand under a higher level of consciousness. And its antithesis is a descending octave—accidental or fated. Without intention, consciousness. It's an entropic process which runs its course and degrades—it's utterly mechanical. It's sort of like the difference between spiritual love and passionate love."

"I think I get it," she said. "Oow, look at that bird, he's beautiful, isn't he?"

"Yeah, he is. How can you tell it's a he?"

"His color. He's a house finch. And I bet he gets all the babes . . . the female finch is a sucker for the brightest and reddest males. It signals fitness."

"The only thing you don't seem to know anything about is Rajingiev . . ." he said.

"Mmm, yes . . . and I *want* to know more about it—"

"All right, well, the law of the octave has a lot of other names: law of seven, law of shock, law of no return—as in Nietzsche's law of return, or eternal recurrence. It explains why things don't just go on and on. Nietzsche, as you know, was basically a determinist, a fatalist. He was saying that if you played it all over again, it would be exactly the same. Every event. But Rajingiev believed if we were careful to interpret the signs and not miss the right moment, at a shock point— a 'mechanical shock' outside of us—it's almost like a wormhole or gateway to a different reality; we can, with our own conscious shock, go through the gate—change things, and bring them to completion.

"Julian's waking you was a shock point. It brought you to madness. The dimension of dreams. For whatever reason, there was some thought or feeling there, you chose to wake up at the shock point, to open the door or gate, and write, instead of going back to sleep, which is what most people would have done. Your conscious shock was writing 'Love Stories.' And 'Love Stories' sent you on a whole new octave ride. The process of writing changed you."

"I'm on an octave ride, huh?"

"That's the way I see it. You're somewhere around *mi*. As in *do re mi*. If you had never written, you might not have ever been open to me. And I would have never read it. And I would probably not be sitting here with you under this maple. You wouldn't be singing. It's like I told you the first day I came over: we choose our fate by where we place our focus—in the form of thought, feeling, emotion, and prayer. That's the conscious shock. There's still a big part of me that believes in fate, though. But the thing of it is, I'm learning, we have some control."

"It sounds a lot like Hegel. Like triadic dialectics. But he doesn't have a third force."

"Right, that makes sense—the western tradition doesn't see past dualism."

"But it's similar to what you're talking about. Thesis is the active first force; and its opposition or contradiction is antithesis, which is your passive, second force. From the resolution of the conflict, you get a new creation: a synthesis. And that synthesis can become a new thesis, which is like the law of the octave. And probably like Rajingiev, the end point is complete perfection."

"Ultimately, yes. You're very beautiful."

They talked like this a lot.

And she realized then that he was third force. Maybe that's one reason he was attracted to this theory. He felt fated to his essence of third force. The catalyst. The seducer. The prophet—the shock. It's not like he didn't observe himself. He *did* his work. He knew what he was. He just didn't much like it. He wanted to be untangled from it. Rajingiev said third could become one. Rajingiev said he could change. Rajingiev said he could transcend. But for now, he could only be Caleb. To woo. With sex energy.

Caleb was her corrective conscious shock.

He was ready to bring the sexuality of their phone conversations into the realm of the physical and their spiritual talks into the realm of the sexual. He was driven to raise the stakes and it was hard to keep up with him. But she had been with her husband for twelve years and had never kissed another man, never even flirted. She had spent that time in guilty seclusion, Rapunzelized.

So he talked a lot about sex energy. About transformation and transcendence through sex. She wasn't ready to sleep with him, though. She didn't trust him enough. She didn't love him. But she didn't want to lose him. And she wanted to love him. Maybe with time and trust she could. But his experience of time was different. It was faster for him. Time was contracted. She knew if she didn't sleep with him that it would be a battle, what evolutionary psychologists call "strategic interference." He'd be angry. He'd be mean. And in the end she'd still be left with the same choice: screw him to get him to be nice again, or lose him. She wasn't ready for battle. To do battle she'd have to care more. She'd have to need him. And she didn't. She wanted to need him. Wanted to need somebody. She had been hurt too much before to need anybody now; she knew she was alone in the end.

But her mind told her a way to the soul (or heart) was through the body. And though her soul wasn't ready, her body was. Or so her mind had thought so.

⌒

It was early November and Julian was visiting his grandparents with his dad. Caleb was at her house. He played his guitar, and she sang. And though she made him dinner, he seemed edgier and was even starting to look different.

"Mmm," he said, as she put the roast chicken and the beans and the artichokes and the small potatoes on the table. "I've never smelled anything so good," he said, though his face was severe.

"Can I get you a glass of wine?" she asked.

"No. No thank you," he said.

And she poured herself a glass and sat with him.

He lowered his head, slightly, to pray.

He seemed to be in another world.

"Can you tell me about that?" she asked, when he came back.

"Sure. What do you want to know?"

"Are you blessing the food? Giving thanks? What?"

"I guess I am. But it's a little more complicated. Don't want to get into it now. But it has to do with *self-remembering*, so I can take in the food and air and impressions and be fully nourished," he said.

"Hmm. I read about a recent study with two-hundred Korean women trying to get pregnant by in vitro—they had people all over the world pray for half of them, without their knowing. Have you heard about that?"

"No."

"It's amazing, really . . . half of the women who were prayed for became pregnant compared to a quarter who weren't prayed for . . ."

"Well, of course. I'm surprised it wasn't more. Prayer is the act of concentrating and directing energy, or emanations— charged-fine-matter . . . But I don't want to talk too much anymore. Too much talk. Your food is too good not to give it our full attention."

"Okay . . ." she said, sort of appreciating this gift of verbal rest. But she also felt a longing for connection with him— alienated . . . awe, too. So they sat there, eating the food in silence; though he ate it better than she.

She got up to get the apple-pear cobbler.

"You didn't want wine with dinner," she said, putting the cobbler down. "How about a glass of really good port?"

"I don't drink. And I don't want you to drink either."

"Oh, Caleb, come on. Are you kidding?"

"No. It's no better than smoking or drugs or any of it. I don't believe in it."

There was obviously a lot here, but in an uncharacteristic move, she decided to leave it alone for the time being. Perhaps because of the tension she felt.

"You look ripe," he told her across the table. She was wearing a tight fitting top and loose jeans.

"I'm going to have some port," she said. "Ripe? Only a hungry man would notice. Or would any man?"

"There's no distinction. All men are hungry," he said seriously. "And I'd rather you not—" he said, standing up and taking the port from her hand, placing it on the table. They felt a heavy force between them, magnetic, electric, pulling.

"Okay, Caleb, okay," she said, about the port. "Then maybe it's just a question of degrees . . . maybe some men are hungrier than others."

"I don't know. I can only really know about *my* hunger," he said.

"Well, would you prefer I appear less so next time?" she asked.

"No. I would prefer you appear no more and no less than as you are."

There was a double meaning in that, of course. He was talking about her essence. But also, something else.

"Appear as *I am?* Then like this?" she asked.

"No. As you *are* . . . Look, I have to leave soon—I've got some work I've got to finish by tomorrow," he told her.

His smile was gone. The only way to soften him, she thought, was with the softness between her legs.

She got up to start clearing and asked him, flirting, but mostly because she wanted to know how to please him, "Do you like my jeans down on my hips, or here, up on my waist?"

He seemed irritated and said tensely, humorlessly, "I like it naked," and got up from the table and walked out the back door to his truck parked in the driveway. She ran outside after him.

"Caleb! C'mon! Come back. Don't be angry." She walked up to him as he was getting into his truck. He got in and sat there, the door open, his right hand on the steering wheel, looking ahead. She stood there calmly and unbuttoned her blouse.

"Caleb, I can be naked," she said softly.

His face and body relaxed, and he pulled her into the truck, kissing her. Then, his hands on her waist, he led her into the house and up the stairs.

"Open your eyes," he said, finally inside her.

She had never felt this connected to a man. It wasn't a connection as ally: (cave)man as meat provider, woman as vessel. It was even older and deeper. It was a Platonic connection, in the philosophical sense. Where anima and animus meet. Where yin and yang fuse. Where light finds darkness. Where there is only essence. He was the "other" and this otherness completed her.

Later she'd come across their looking-into-one-another's-eyes, for extended amounts of time during sex, as a technique, one maybe he had learned. The technique's called *karezza*, also *magnetation*. When your eyes are open—locked—you can't help but feel connected to the primal, the universal. It's a spiritual feeling—timeless, yet bound to nature and life itself. How can you see into your lover's soul and find completion there if your eyes are closed? Anyway, it had too many elements of the feminine for it to have been a natural instinct, to have come from his core—his masculine, animal nature. It was about helping him transcend. It was about his heart and soul, not just his dick. But it also enabled his masculine principle to be seen and felt. And it was a gift, because it's what a woman wants.

She felt fulfilled deeply, essentially, but oddly, because she wasn't ready, something felt missing. Without time and trust, she could not fully open to him. Without opening to him, he would soon leave. He needed her to be right there with him, and she couldn't be.

But her heart *was* opening, it was just slow. She was looking into his eyes and wishing she were eighteen again. He was giving her the world and love with his eyes.

"I can't believe you—you're—what am I going to do with you?" she said.

"Shh! Spit in my mouth when you come," he said to her as he moved her on top of him, getting her to sit up.

"You're beautiful," he said, holding her breasts.

"You are, too," she said. He pulled on her hair. He didn't want to come, he believed it took away life, he believed it was removed from transcendence, but he couldn't help it, he told her he loved her and came.

But she didn't. And wouldn't throughout the affair.

Caleb understood her unresponsiveness as his failure, but in fact, sex was more pleasurable for her when her focus was in her chest and not between her legs. The sexual act was an expression of her love. But she could not both feel love and take. She could only be taken and love, give and love. It was a lesson learned preverbally, or prenatally, maybe even prehistorically. It couldn't be undone and she didn't want it undone. Biopsychoenergetics wasn't going to work for this modern hysteric. Her heart and root chakras, as Caleb might say, were disconnected permanently.

She was stuck between root and heart. Somewhere in her gut. Between strategies. To feel in her heart, she'd have to negate below. To feel down below, she'd need to negate her heart. But her heart was more important to her than her sex (getting off was easy) and her heart was beginning to move, to feel, to open like a flower. And it was fighting. Love and sex pushing against each other, she could feel it. The blood, the chi. A cool tingling above her navel.

But this battle of the organs had nothing to do with the fact that when her heart won—it only won briefly—that it couldn't feel for more than a second or two at a time. This was the hardest fight. Opening to love. (Or maybe it was about trust.)

They lay in bed on their sides, facing each other, each trying to operate as the other, he as feminine, she as masculine. For her, as defense, for him, transcendence. For survival. He said, "I was supposed to meet you. . . . It's like I'm following my path. And I see us together, here, in this house. Do you see it? I see it. It feels like I'm remembering, but it's the future."

She wondered if he was, consciously or not, giving her what he knew she wanted. Because he read "Love Stories." It was Sarah, her character from "soft kill," who said that when a man played the fate card, he always won her. But she knew Caleb truly worked this way, despite his not wanting to, just as she did, romantically, mystically.

"I do. I felt it from the beginning, you know that. I tried to resist it. I've waited so long for you. What took you so long?"

"I'm here now," he said.

"But now I'm damaged. And I'm—I don't think you can wait for me to heal."

"I want you to feel. I want you to heal," he said.

He moved his hand to her chest and caressed it. They lay there for a while like that.

She suspected these romantic fate thoughts they both had were "designed" for a reason. That there had to be some kind of belief-in-fate module, a mental organ in the brain, just as there is a belief-in-God module. Some people's are "set" very high. Others don't even have them. Perhaps this fate module was even close to the God module, some kind of Belief area, maybe near the amygdala or hypothalamus.

"Caleb, I think this fate idea, or feeling that we have, is some kind of mechanical, deep evolutionary thing. You can see the value as far as reproduction, right? . . . Our ancestors who had thoughts like this were probably tenacious . . . and could beat out their rivals for their desired mate . . . and would care for their loved offspring in a passionate way. *The survival of the belief-in-fate* gene."

She hated doing this to herself, to him. Analyzing it. Taking the beauty out of it. The mystery. Turning the spiritual into the material. Being left with genes instead of love.

But her analysis didn't really take it away. It was still there. She still felt it.

"Yes, I have the fate module . . . the believe-in-fate module, whatever. And I'm glad it's there. But it *is* mechanical; I believe in something much higher. Conscious love. Attention."

And then they kissed and kissed and kissed.

Caleb knew then it would happen. Their collective vision, their foreseen future, sealed with their lips, was all that was needed. The fates could be tempted, ridiculed even. He would soon live with his love.

# *heliotrope*

They are trying to become one creature, and something will
not have it . . . They feel themselves at the center of a
powerful and baffled will.                              —*Robert Hass*

The Seduction of Odysseus
To navigate the waters of desire
tie him down but let him hear
a crew which cannot hear
a traveler who cannot move
put into service what you must
for the will
it needs wax and ropes
to steer away
the siren's song
                              —*C. L. Jones*

Our sun is a delicate balance of two opposing forces: gravity
and the nuclear force. Without the nuclear force, gravity
would crush it, without gravity, the sun would be blown
apart.                                        —*Michio Kaku*

Havtha Studios was a beautiful two hundred and thirty-three-
year-old farm house, eight miles outside of town in the mountains. It was here that they spent much of their time. The
house had been willed to Heliosen by an eccentric sculptor
for the express purpose of "seeking the spiritual in art." It was
Caleb who had the idea to turn the old house into a music
company and so Havtha was born. Caleb and others from the
community converted it into sound and recording rooms, an
office, a rehearsal space, a gallery for exhibiting visual art, a

kitchen, and a meditation/yoga room. There was even an out-
door sauna which Caleb had built, in the Finnish style, with a
sod roof and cold dipping pool. On their walks out there
from Havtha, Caleb would take the lead and she would fol-
low behind him about three feet. The etiology of this seemed
innocent enough. One day Caleb got an early start and she
could never quite catch up to him. But then, it happened
again. Until finally, that was their habit. They never spoke
about it. They felt the rightness of it to their core. It was a
walking dance which fulfilled something ancient and primal
for them and though both understood the sexist implications,
they didn't care, not here.

Before rehearsing a song he had commanded her to write,
on an instrument she could barely play, and which, despite
herself, she wrote, they sat in the meditation room, on yoga
blankets, in the middle of the floor. This was an addition to
the farmhouse and light came in from everywhere, from the
skylights, from the massive windows and sliding doors. Sitting there they felt the weight of their actions but they felt
the lightness, the ease of it, too.

"I told him," she said.

"You did," he said, intrigued.

"Yeah. Now we'll see what's fueling this thing, right? I mean,
I just didn't want us to be getting off on the forbidden-ness of it.
I want it to be pure. And he needed to know," she said.

"I understand. And how did he take it?"

"Quite well. He's either shocked and it'll hit him in a few
days or . . . I don't know. He says he loves me and wants me
to be happy and he's going to give me space. It's . . . He
doesn't seem jealous at all. You're more jealous than he is.
Even when I tell you there's no reason for it, that I haven't
touched him in half a year, that I'm not interested in my col-

leagues or men on the streets or my next door neighbor. I guess it tells me how you both feel about me. Or maybe just what kind of men you are. He's not really a jealous type."

"I am jealous. I am very jealous," he said, almost sad.

"I know, Caleb. I love your jealousy. I think it's beautiful, though it's unsettling," she said.

"I hate it," he said.

"Don't hate it. It's a survival mechanism. As long as you're not hitting men in bars, you're fine. You know what evolutionary psychologists think about it, right?"

"No, baby, I don't."

"It's an anti-cuckoldry thing. It's this strong emotion for a reason—when you're screwing someone you need to be sure of your paternity, otherwise you could end up raising some other guy's kid."

"And that will never happen, unless I want it to," he said.

"I think that's true. Did you notice when Lily was first born—people told you she looked like you?"

"Yeah, and it's funny 'cause I only saw Kate in her."

"That's interesting . . . well, there's this social psychologist who says babies have evolved to resemble their fathers. On the savannah, in the EEA, the more certain the father was of his paternity, the better care the child got, presumably. Survival of the *resemblance* gene."

He watched her move her hair from her face.

"I like your mouth. It's beautiful."

"Thank you," she smiled.

"It's possible the resemblance thing might just be a social phenomena though—conscious or unconscious—a way family and community mollify the father to ensure he takes care of the child. The point is, jealousy fuels behavior to prevent the woman you're with from being with anyone other than you. It's your biological destiny, Caleb. You can't be unfettered. Rajingiev can't help you. And I tell you what, I think you've got an extra dose of it. But it's 'cause your ancestors were quite successful. All those men before you probably raised their own kin. It's in your blood, you're an alpha."

"You make it sound good, but it feels like shit."

"It's supposed to feel like shit—until you do what your selfish genes want you to do." Caleb was working on the tension he felt inside, his discomfort with her knowledge, her display of it. She saw the tension on his face.

"You don't want to hear about this evolutionary—this EP stuff, do you?"

"Actually, I do, very much," he said. But he wanted to say, *I do, but I'm not used to women knowing anything more than I do. It intimidates me and I don't like that it does and I don't understand it.* While in the depths of his cortical layers were the images: her behind, with her panties at her knees and her knees on the ground, in her, in her very small hole, the back of her head.

She went on tentatively, "Okay, well, we have emotions for a reason. They make us act. The good ones push us on our course, making us strive for more; the bad and sad ones, if we listen, make us stop, and ultimately change our strategies. My fear is that your Rajingiev ride is about learning how not to feel the bad and sad ones."

His impulse was to interrupt; he thought she was wrong about Rajingiev. But he didn't.

"This shit is deep, Caleb. We're talking millions and millions of years of evolution. It's a brilliant thing, jealousy. But it's true, like any emotion that serves a valuable purpose for the individual or his genes, it can stick around long after its usefulness. It's just that jealousy feels useful to the atavistic part of you."

"I'm not following you. But maybe I don't want to. No, that's not true. Explain it."

"Okay. Despite my every effort to convince you nothing is going on with my husband, you continue to feel jealous. And that is because, I think, you need to see him physically leave my orbit. Now most men would trust my words. But you, you probably pick up his pheromones. And you know I spend time with him. And your reptilian brain, the hunter-Pleistocene part of you, cannot reconcile that this male is ever near me. Your deep part doesn't trust me. And it's in conflict with your neocortex. Because you believe me, at least at the symbolic level of language, you believe me. But the words are meaningless to the hunter. He wants to see blood."

"I think you may be right," he said, "but I also think 'the work' helps me control this apeman. Most people go around asleep, reacting without any understanding. My work is about waking up; it's not about not feeling bad. Essence is beyond all this. It's beyond evolution. You think this EP theory is the end-and-be-all, it's not. Besides, there's studies out there showing that at the individual level, the genetic code is variable, it's not fixed. You can turn shit on and off. There are real scientists, sweetie, who think we can change, mutate, at the genetic level. It's like the choices we make in our lives can change the condition of our bodies. I know. You're gonna say Lamarck."

She didn't want to argue or debate. She never wanted to with him. Anyway, she was always able to see his side of things and she was glad. They seemed to believe different things, but at the core, she thought, they were the same.

"You know what I feel now?" he half whispered, half groaned.

"What?" she mirrored his tone.

"I feel like—like lying down with you naked," he said.

She stretched her body out and lay on her side. He gazed at her and stood and said, "But we shouldn't. I think it's the perfect time for us to do the music. I can make love to you—

by playing your music. I want to put the energy there. I want to hear your song. I want to learn how to play it for you. That's what I want to do."

"It's called sublimation," she said wryly.

"That's one term for it. Esoterics have others. You call it what you want. I like to think of it as the most primary energy we have—sex energy—transforming into a higher energy—art energy—Art—in this case music. It's part of my practice. You know why? There's lots of reasons. But let me give you one: this damn hunter you talk about, this ancient Plasticene—"

"Pleistocene," she corrected softly.

"Try not to interrupt me," he said, seriously.

"I'm sorry," she said, feeling like maybe she was interrupting again.

"It's okay. But just listen. Really listen . . . Listen like you were going to have to repeat what I say. . . . This hunter wants you all the time. Sometimes more than other times, but it's this constant desire. He wants to be inside you, in any hole he can get into . . . And if he could, that's all he would do. He would just fuck you . . . and fuck you . . . and fuck you . . . And he'd never let you near another man. Do you have any understanding of that?" he asked rhetorically not waiting for an answer. "No, of course not," he said. He reached down with his arm to pull her up, "Come on baby, let me hear your song."

They walked to the main part of the farmhouse and into the studio. She picked up a guitar and sang him her song:

*I'd been waiting so long for you/I am cold and numb and confused/Why'd you take so long to find me here my love/I'm not sure if I can love/For the love you gave/For the love we made/ I'm not sure if you can wait/For me to open now/Like a lotus flower/to give my nectar away . . .*

His eyes were teary. She wondered if he had always been able to do that or if his "work" had helped him to be able to do it. Teary on him seemed so misplaced, and that made it all the more beautiful.

She taught him the chords and he played while she sang. They worked on the song for hours. While he played she said, "I hear voices. I hear voices coming out."

And she did. When Caleb played, truth, beauty and the good met in the heavens and you could hear angels.

After, they went to the kitchen and she made them a quick couscous and chick pea dish. Neither had eaten the whole day and the simple dish she had prepared was, at first, manna. By the second bowlful it was couscous and chickpeas. He went to the refrigerator and pulled out an exotic Indian chutney.

"Try some, sweetie," he said.

"Oh, no thanks," she said.

"Come on, please have some."

"No, no thanks," she said again.

"It's really good, though, you should try it."

"I really don't want chutney now, Caleb."

"But it's great—Ted brought it back from India last month. Just try it."

"No. I don't want any. Thank you."

"Come on, have some," he pleaded.

"What is your deal? Is this some kind of Rajingiev exercise?"

"No. In fact, very much not. I just want you to try it. It's good for you. It'll make you strong."

"I don't want any, Caleb. My stomach does not want chutney. What is it that you aren't understanding? I don't want any chutney, but thank you!"

"Oh, come on, just a tiny bit," he said trying to charm her with his beautiful, intense eyes.

She was so exhausted by this hypnotic, neurotic, controlling mind fuck at this point and realized he was not going to let up, so she had an idea: "Okay, well, if you really want me to eat it because it'll make you feel better . . ."

"No, it's okay," he said. And both were satisfied.

And then if that wasn't mad enough he said, "Were you doing anything just before to affect me?"

"What do you mean?" she asked. "Do you mean was I purposively being seductive?"

He gave her a wink, nodded, and smiled.

"No," she said, incredulous.

"Are you sure?" He seemed paranoid, suspicious, as if her femininity were calculated. He might as well have called her a temptress. Caleb had his own struggles with women, with mama.

"Yes, I'm sure."

"You didn't do *anything* to get me?"

"Well, I don't know. When I took my sweater off, I did feel your eyes on me and that made me feel sexy, but—"

"Aha."

"But it's more like you make me feel sexy—it's not to affect you—not on purpose. Maybe it's that your presence and your energy affect me without my knowledge. I'm not trying to be sexy, Caleb," she said earnestly. She wanted to say something funny but she knew to try to lighten him would only make him feel heavier.

Something deeper was at work beyond her will, she knew, but he didn't believe her. In spite of himself, Caleb loved her. He felt like she was like all the women he had loved. Beautiful and powerful—able to make him want to drag her down to the ground—to waste precious seed—at the slightest sensual gesture. He was intrigued by the affect these women had on him. What was it exactly that stirred him? Why did he

want to fuck her so badly even when he "knew" she was "working it"? He vowed he'd work on that troubling aspect about
himself in his Tuesday yurt sessions with Ted, Heliosen's brilliant and charismatic founder and guru.

They sat for a while in a window seat, in the kitchen, holding each other—her head on his chest, his hand going through
her hair—daydreaming together.

"I'm damaged, Caleb. You shouldn't love me. I want to open
. . . to open my heart. I can't."

He put his hand on her chest and rubbed it hoping to
open her.

"I'm a magician," he told her, gravelly and deep.

Coming from anyone else, this three-word avowal would
have seemed stilted and ridiculous. But he believed it and so
did she.

"I *want* to give myself to you . . ." she said.

"And I want to give yourself to you," he told her.

For a moment her heart opened.

She asked, "Are you Erich or Finn?"

"I'm not sure I'm either."

She hoped he'd be Finn. She wanted a happy ending. But she
had her doubts.

"You know, I could listen to your voice for a lifetime," she
said. "And your smell—it's intoxicating—it calms me and ex-
cites me at the same time, making me want more. And your
mind—I like the contents of it—enough to go with, enough to
resist. And I like the way it works—your intelligence with your
strange manipulative, insecure, secretive, magical, deep way turns
me on. And your soul. Dark. Fiery. Powerful. Weak. Lusty.
Hungry. And I think you're beautiful. The little boy. Your pain,
your goodness, and the bad. Your search. I mean, I find you,
your core, or essence, difficult to resist, even though . . ." She
looked out the window, slightly shaking her head.

"Even though what?" he asked.

"I don't know—even though maybe I should."

He put her hair behind her ear and said, "Don't resist me," and he kissed her neck.

They continued to sit silently caressing each other; then she sat up straight and said out of the blue, "Caleb, why is it that you've only brought me to Heliosen once?"

Caleb shifted his back to the corner wall. "The truth is, sweetie, when I met you I had been seeing someone. Her name's Claudia."

"Oh," she felt panic and relief at the same time.

"How long have you been with her?" she asked in the present tense.

"We had been together for about three months when I met you. I haven't exactly told her about us yet because I don't want to hurt her. She lives in the community and I want to stay her friend," he said.

"Are you still seeing her?"

"No. The whole time I was with her I thought I must have transcended. 'The death of desire is the death of the individual.' You wrote that, remember?"

"Actually, I didn't write it. It's a quote from the *New York Times*. But yes, it's in 'Love Stories.'"

"That's what I want. The death of the individual. To go beyond 'personality.' To transcend. And I thought it had happened. I thought, 'this is young to have begun to transcend through sex energy,' but I accepted it."

At bottom they wanted the same thing. To be saved. To be free. They just had opposing strategies, principles. Whereas she thought the way to freedom was in turning the volume of life up, he thought it was in turning it down. She was after desire. To be attached to life. He, ultimately, wanted to be free of desire: non-attachment.

"And then one day I was in the city and it came back to me," he said.

"There's nothing like a day in SoHo to cure a blocked libido," she said.

He smiled at her. He knew she wanted to lighten him—to make him less serious. And he liked that she tried.

"And then I saw you. And it was more than just libido. It was that and more instantly. I've never felt that way for Claudia. But I can't tell her yet."

"So what does she think then? What have you told her?" she asked.

"She thinks I'm going through a strange time—which I am. And that I can't deal with externals right now—which is also sort of true."

"Aren't I an 'external'?" she asked, half-seriously.

"You, you don't feel like an external. You feel very much a part of me," he said.

She still didn't understand. She told her *husband!* But she felt she had more power in the relationship and so she let him be mysterious. She didn't question him; she let him keep the back door open for Claudia though he was saying otherwise. Later she'd understand this and wonder, *Was he aware of what he was doing? Or was it unconscious?*

⌒

It was Saturday evening and Julian had spent the day with his father. Now she would go home to make dinner for them though things were unbearably strained, painfully tense between them. They did this for Julian. To keep the semblance of family. It wasn't a back door, but Caleb thought so. And he was angry.

"Look, I hate ultimatums but you have to get out of your marriage or I can't be with you," he said to her.

She didn't understand the rush. *Why so drastic? What is he trying to do?* She didn't want to lose him so she talked to her husband that evening about Caleb's ultimatum. She didn't say what she wanted. She didn't know. It did not go over well.

"It's one thing for this asshole to have an affair and screw my wife," he told her. "It's another thing to take my wife—to replace me!"

All of this was not new to him. They had been living with her unhappiness for years. Years before, when Julian was four, she had asked for a divorce, but he begged her to stay. She told him it was inevitable and that to prolong it would only be more damaging for their son—the older he got the more hurtful. He didn't cry that time but somehow he convinced her not to leave. They had had passion at one time. They had felt forms of jealousy and sexual longing many years before. But those feelings were probably based on times when one wasn't as desirous as the other—an ego-driven passion. It had never been—and both always recognized this—a deep love—souls recognizing, scents knowing, bodies understanding.

## the fate of icarus

It was a fight to the death between them—or to new life:
though in what the conflict lay, no one could say.
—*D. H. Lawrence*

> Odysseus
> There were the islands
> Each with its woman and twining welcome
> To be navigated, and one to call "home."
> The knowledge of all that he betrayed
> Grew till it was the same whether he stayed
> or went.
> —*W.S. Merwin*

Caleb's demands were beginning to weaken her. His pushing her to leave her husband seemed to push *him* out. She began to forget with him. Everything Caleb said seemed to float away. There was nowhere in her gray matter for it to stick. And she didn't understand, couldn't control it. She *wanted* to remember. The things he told her, the things that happened, were important to her. But she kept forgetting. Where was her memory? Where was it all going?

And her body. It was trying to protect her from him.

Her heart was closed from so much hurt before him that it would not open. Not enough. And there were reasons not to trust him. And now, she began to *feel* the pressure on her to leave her husband. She began to somaticize. She couldn't speak, couldn't remember. Language, memory, gone. Her body's language taking over, telling her what she couldn't say. What she didn't want to say. Because she wanted to be with him. The body that wanted to melt into him closed. All the little negatives about him started to add up and her heart couldn't take it. His velocity. His controlling way. His too thin legs. His lying. His disdain for academia. His innate amorality. His darkness. His Heliosen life. His unknowns. There *was* a math to it.

Her heart was trying so hard to open, wanting to—the mind, the soul. But the body saying no. An ache in her upper right back that felt nauseated. A cool, tingly feeling in her gut rising up making her heart feel cool, clogged, numb. A feeling of wanting to open her mouth to let the cool, gauzy feeling out. A need to run.

Caleb told her he thought it was because she felt guilt. She told him she knew it wasn't. She didn't feel guilt and she barely felt guilt for not feeling guilt. It was him. He had wanted her, her whole life then and there. She couldn't do it for so many reasons.

Because she was conflicted, she unconsciously began to move away from him, slowly. It was the way she had wanted to move toward him, but he would not let her. As it was, she had a habit of truth-telling which bordered on the perverse. It was a simulacra. It was post-postmodern. She played with it, watching its social effect. She knew that seduction was not about truth. She knew that to demystify herself would be unattractive. To play the game of seduction is serious. It says, I have everything to lose and everything to gain, and I will dissemble and hide and disappear and lie and intrigue and mystify, in the hope of seducing you, because I want to possess you. Not to play the game is to affirm the opposite: to say, I have power, and I don't need you and I don't want to possess you. And though this can be attractive, it is not seductive. (It's also a strategy of the weak, the fearful seducer.)

Her unconscious knew what it was doing: it was pushing him away. When he asked her if she dyed her hair, she was happy to tell him the truth, even though she knew it bothered him. (She wondered why high-testosterone males had such a finely-tuned deception radar. Her husband didn't care at all about such things.) The more Caleb seduced and negated and hid, the more she disclosed, demystified—to kill her desire, to kill his.

She did it with sex, too. Even when there was no desire, she gave in to him. This worked to fill him up until he didn't want anymore. Her honesty here would have created more desire in him. It would have seduced. So she drowned him in the lie of her flesh. She created abundance until there was no hunger left.

~

She was having that bad feeling in her chest again.

While she read and graded final papers for her philosophy course, the one she had been teaching lately as if an afterthought, Caleb pulled into her driveway like a madman. She sat there, stiff, remembering several papers she had done as a college student, the ones with nary a comment, but a big A at the top, and understanding.

She went to the porch. He stood on the grass. "Hi. I'm grading papers. What's up?"

"Can I come in?"

"Actually, I need to get out."

And she closed the door behind her without locking it and they walked to his car.

When she got in the car he asked, "Why are you killing that ficus?"

She looked toward her back yard and felt ashamed but defended herself and rescued the sad poetry.

"I'm not killing it. Its leaves had all fallen off so I'm keeping it out here for the winter. It'll come back in the spring."

"I'm not so sure," he said.

"No, it will, you'll see."

"I don't think it works with those kind of trees," he said.

"It does. It will . . . Whose car is this?" she asked.

"It's mine."

It was as run down and unpretentious as his truck, and he drove it in a way that frazzled her nerves and touched her heart. She wouldn't figure out until later, but Claudia, it seems, was driving his truck.

They went walking in the cool mountains. She still felt conflicted. She wanted him, but not the way he needed her to. She couldn't just get out of her twelve-year marriage, with a son, for a man she knew for a few months. She was doing the best she could, but it wasn't enough for him.

Finally it started to make sense to her. The rush to commit. It was the hunter in him. His atavistic need to be the only man in her contact. A disabled forebrain. There were other reasons probably, but every time she thought about them they frustrated her, like the possibility he had his damn astrological chart read which told him he'd have to commit to someone before the new year. Or that he was following the credo "focus, take aim and commit to love" too intently without listening to her, without listening to himself. Or that he had been trying to give her her story. He had read "Love Stories," after all. The quick and romantic flight into Finn's arms and life.

Later she'd write about and understand Caleb's haste in the context of value, focus, strategy, and time.

She was watching three rock climbers rappel down a cliffside as she and Caleb walked along a carriage road.

"I came back down to earth," she told him.

"What did you say?"

"I came back down to earth."

For Caleb this was more than an expression. Though he wasn't a fanatic follower of Rajingiev, when he heard these words he knew it was all over for both of them. They would not transcend. The laws that governed them on earth would continue to weigh them down. They were too far away from where he wanted to go. He glared up at the sun, looked suspiciously at her, and got his armor ready. The hunt over, he'd now prepare for battle. He told himself, *Blood is going to spill, and it won't be mine.*

She tried to be light, she was just talking. She didn't think she wanted to push him away. "You should be with a girl in her twenties who will do anything you want and worship you. And I should probably be with some exceedingly wealthy guy in his fifties." She believed the part about him, but not for her. She didn't know what she wanted anymore, but an older man wasn't exactly humming for her, despite what the evolutionary psychologists she read said. *Maybe it's their old, wishful thinking*, she thought.

The gauziness was gone. And the coolness, too. But her chest still felt tight and so did her back. Caleb was hurt but feigned the lightness with her.

"If that's the way you feel, I think we should try to be friends. We should try to do the music, that's it."

"Okay," she said. She felt rejected, and sad, though she knew she had forced him to this. "It's you now, you're the one saying this, so, you have to keep your word that you won't grab me during rehearsals. It's not fair."

She had almost forgotten that two weeks earlier at Havtha,

they had come to this same decision, haphazardly, and, while playing together, on the very day they said they would just be friends, he was compelled to make love to her. And she was compelled to let him.

"I'm going to try," he said.

"That's not good enough. If we say this, then we have to stick to it," she said, smiling, "otherwise let's not say it."

"Okay," he said, "I'll keep my word."

On their way back to the car she watched the same climbers from before start up the same cliffside and she thought, *Maybe the ache is fear. Maybe I'm afraid to love.* Her ache was almost gone, but now she felt empty. She realized she was going to lose him. She didn't know how much longer he'd stay. She had nothing to offer him anymore. She would have continued to give her body to him, but he had raised the stakes. "If you don't get out of your marriage, I can't be with you." The body was no longer enough. And it seemed to her that her "non-seduction strategy" worked, that he had lost feeling for her, too.

She knew he didn't need her voice—the recording, the "rehearsals" were a gift to her, and a way to legitimately see her. (After her husband knew of their affair, Caleb still used the music as a cover. *Was he protecting my reputation?* she wondered. The realization would come to her at the kitchen sink: of course! It was a cover for Claudia—in case Lily said something to her, in case she saw them together, in case.)

In the car, it was hard for them not to notice their own bodies. Sometimes they moved with the car, other times against it. They were trying to keep themselves from touching one another and it wasn't always easy with some of those mountainous curves, with that kinetic energy. They were still both *attracted* to each other. It would have been so easy just to reach over, for either of them, *and kiss and kiss and kiss.*

(The car to the side of the road, of course.) But they promised they would be good. They would stick to their plan.

In their weighty regret, both feeling like they wanted to go home and cry, they decided to stop at an old salvage place that Caleb had been telling her about for weeks, because he knew she was looking for a tub. And he knew she would love the old barn.

Inside, they walked past antique doors—some with stained glass, mantels, and large brackets for porches—until they got to what were probably hundreds of old porcelain sinks and tubs. Naturally, she felt a lift.

They surveyed the old basins, and as they looked at each, she realized that her cognitive process was deep. She was rather picky, rather choosy: the faucet wasn't the right shape, the chrome on the handles too worn or not worn enough, the white of the porcelain the wrong hue. She knew there were plenty of men who probably walked in there and, if the tub was the right size, bought it. But she was a woman. It had to do with the algorithms of her adapted brain. Females choose males. They gather and weed. They choose, if they can, the best males. The sublime. Because it's the old story: if they're not careful, if they don't choose well, it's nine months . . . it's a lifetime . . .

And suddenly—it was the way he looked at her—as she was rejecting one tub after another, she understood. Caleb was exacerbated by the process. It wore him down. It took a lot of energy to be both turned on and turned off by her particularness. That's what was going on in him.

The part that was turned on by her choosiness (it didn't matter that they were saying they were over) was so for two important reasons: one, her choosiness was a good indication she'd reject other men's sexual invitations; and two, she would probably pass this trait on to their daughter, if they ever had one, which would ensure a fit male for his grandchildren, and ultimately his descendants. This wasn't conscious, of course.

The other part, a darker side maybe, was turned off by a choosy woman. This part sought women who could commit soon and without a *but*. A woman who did that made life easy. She wouldn't be much of a cost. It wasn't because Caleb was a bad guy. It was an old, deep reflex.

She too felt a contradiction within her. In part, she didn't want any of those tubs, but she also struggled against her discerning impulse. It was a natural struggle. Both strategies were there. It was something most every woman in history has had to do at one point: be practical. Commit. Choose. With limited time and knowledge. Anyway, there is a math to this. A woman can look at the first fourteen percent of candidates—bathtubs, men—and have an eighty-three percent chance of finding a tub or man in the top ten percent. If she's good.

So not knowing which part of her was talking to which part of him, she said, "That one. That one's fine. It's got a chip in it, but as long as everything else is all right, it's fine."

Was she saying this to push him away, or because she still wanted him? She really didn't want that imperfect tub, and he knew it. So with this, there was a sense she was past telling truths that would turn him off and was now faking to make herself *unattractive* to him—or to the part of him who preferred choosey. They were over, sure, but not really; they had to unravel themselves, each in their own way.

Maybe she *was* saying she wanted him. She sure didn't love that tub though. And through her lack of passion for it, her throwing up her arms as if in defeat, like she didn't have the energy to fight or wait for something better, like she would settle for its imperfection and make it suffer by trying to fix it, she was telling him, I will choose you, *but* . . . There was a conditional implied there, a feeling of doom.

"Really?" he said. "You don't want that tub." He was surprised. Why would she settle for a chip? Was *he* a fine tub with a chip? Was she not so wonderful after all? *She did give-in to sex pretty early.* (No matter what Caleb believed about her, the hunter in him equated yielding-to-sex-early-on as a particular strategy, one that said she wasn't as valuable because she didn't wait to see about other mates, she didn't wait for more signals of investment from him.) In evolutionary psychology, there's a name for her mating strategy: it's called short term. The same went for Caleb, of course.

"Why not? It's fine. It's the best one here. I don't want to keep looking anymore, I just want to get it and be done with it." Every word they said then, which she would later remember, felt surreal and essential.

She was kind, that was her problem. It was so hard to say no. A final no. She didn't want to say a final no. And *maybe* wasn't an option—not for Caleb, whose doors closed so fast.

Is this confusing? Yes, it's confusing. They were confused. They were still together. Nothing really changed, certainly not their feelings. Only their focus—their decision to be friends. They both knew that could change at any moment.

The pushing and pulling inside each of them was a physical thing. Bosons and leptons, maybe even Higgs, had them finally whirling in a clumsy unsynchronized dance which had no rhyme or reason; they were pulled in toward each other, they were pushed apart, now one was in, now one was out. Their gears were off, their algorithms. It was chaos.

"Why don't you wait to find what you're looking for?" he said.

"Nah, this is good enough, and it's really the best one here. I can fix the chip."

"I'm not so sure."

"I can . . . I think. There's this porcelain stuff, they've got it at Ace, I've seen it."

"I think you should wait. They get tubs in here all the time. And there's a place on Route Three that has tubs you should check out."

(Part of him was telling her, *It's okay. Do what your heart tells you, I'm a bad boy.*)

"Okay, maybe you're right," she said, as sadness filled up the empty feeling she had had ever since their walk in the mountains, like osmosis.

So, she didn't buy the tub with the chip, the tub she didn't love, the tub which was just fine. She sort of wanted to, though. She wanted to try to salvage *something*. Maybe. Or maybe she was trying to make it easier for him and harder for her. Just the way she wanted it.

◠

A week later, as planned, Caleb picked her up on his way to Havtha. They had scheduled a three-hour rehearsal from four until seven, which, at the last minute he changed so it would end at six, cutting their time down to two hours. It hurt her because she knew how important it was for him to keep his word. There was significance there, she knew.

It had been a few days since they had run in to each other dropping their kids off at the school. They had walked to her house in the snow, talking and sometimes silent. When they got there he walked her onto the porch. Unexpectedly he said, "I'm so hot for your sweet ass. You're so beautiful, do you know that? I'm engorged for you."

*Engorged?* she said to herself. She had thought he had lost interest in her and had been feeling bad about herself since their walk in the mountains. And what a word.

It went against their plan, their word—to be friends—but she told him he could come in. He said, "No. I better not." And then he left.

She stepped into her house and stood there trying to understand him. Was it he had finally lost attraction but was testing her to see if she was still attracted to him, to see if they *could* be friends? Did he want her, but then had realized it'd still be the same situation? Was he just keeping his word? She was confused. She was more removed than ever from what she felt or what she wanted.

Caleb and Drew spent almost an hour pushing buttons and switching on switches, tuning guitars and checking sounds. It seemed out of the ordinary to her. But she just sat, a little angry, listening to their prattle, watching them do technical things she didn't understand. She felt as if they were buying time—or wasting hers. And she felt like she was twenty again—being the good little girlfriend, quiet, powerless, ineffective. It was clear then to her that she and Caleb were stuck in post-adolescence. They had begun their descent. They had started out together as adults but they were regressing faster and faster. In no time, she suspected, they would behave like adolescents, then children, and soon after, as infantalized preverbal beings, until finally, they would separate into their own wombs.

"It's almost five o'clock, Caleb. We only have about an hour and fifteen minutes now."

He looked seriously at her and said, "I can do a lot in an hour and fifteen minutes."

And Drew said, not missing the sexual innuendo, "Hey, now!" And she thought to herself, *it's true, he can*, remembering a particular time they made love in her attic when they had about that much time before they picked up their children at school.

They had never mentioned her not climaxing. He'd never said, but she knew it upset him. She knew no matter what she told him it wouldn't have made a difference, though. Again, it was deep and evolutionary and she knew it. The female orgasm helps sperm swiftly travel to the egg, it hastens implantation—it might even be a qualitatively different kind of sperm. And probably, men who felt a deep and strong desire to see "their woman" come, sired more children, were philoprogenitive. The survival of the *male coveting female climax* gene.

Caleb began by asking her to play the guitar. She didn't like playing the guitar, though he had taught her some chords. It never felt right to her.

"I want you to play that song you wrote," he said.

"Oh. I really don't want to, Caleb. I thought I was going to sing some of the songs we've been working on. I don't want to play the guitar."

"Oh, c'mon, just play it."

"I really don't want to. Let's just sing the songs. And you play. Please?"

"Just play the damn thing, all right?" he demanded.

She felt masculated. She did not want this phallic extension, this wood nymph to play, like a man plays a woman. Though her soul resisted, her mind knew the image of her with that guitar would help him to reject her.

"What do you think of female guitarists, Drew?" she asked, knowing the answer.

"I don't like them," he said, matter-of-factly.

Caleb said, "I'm intimidated by them." And she knew what that meant.

She began to play her song.

"Are you taping this? Please don't tape it. Okay?" she said casually and almost flirtatiously.

They had had these discussions before. Drew and Caleb had often told each other and other artists that they weren't recording when they were. It was playful. Caleb had a reputation for experimenting with recording. He found spontaneous and unself-conscious music to be "higher." The conscious mental representations, processes, defenses, that the artist goes through when she knows she's being recorded drain her creative energy. "It's left brain versus right brain, man," Drew would say. Something is lost. What Caleb was after was a "higher product."

Caleb, who'd been working out the calculus of them the whole time, exploded. He tore right into her, yelling, "Don't fucking worry about it. I'm just doing a 'scratch.' Just sing, damn it. Look all I've done for you and you don't even realize . . . You can't even act professionally. . . . Don't act so pathetic."

And then, looking down, he said slowly, bitterly, as if under his breath but so she and Drew could both hear, "Fuc . . . king cunt."

"What? What are you talking about? I don't—I just asked you not to tape me. Why are you so upset?"

He looked at her with pure disdain. He was cold and silent.

"I'm leaving!" she said, as she stood up, surprised at her own avowal.

"Fine," he said, not looking up at her.

She put on her coat and stood near the door waiting for him to move.

"Caleb, take me home. Please."

"No!"

"Why not?"

"If you want to leave then go."

"You drove me here, remember? Please take me home."

"No."

"Look, you're the one being the prick—please, take me home."

"If you want me to take you home you'll have to wait until six."

"Why?"

"Because that's when we said we'd finish."

"Well, actually we were supposed to finish at seven, but you changed it to six, remember? So what does it matter now? Why keep our word? You already broke it."

She was thinking he was playing with the law of seven, the law of shock, but she couldn't figure it out.

"That's not the point."

"I don't understand you. Take me home. Please. You should."

"No. I'm a prick, remember?"

"Even pricks can redeem themselves!"

That line, her own words, abstracted—extracted her from the scene. For the first time since that day in the school hallway with him, she had some objectivity. She could see it some. The absurdity of it. And she half-liked uttering the "prick redemption" line. She thought she had finally met her all-or-nothing, passionate match—a man who'd spar with her, who'd get into melodrama, even if it seemed beneath them and belonging in a dorm room.

But Caleb did not respond. He was not about to let this emotion stick around long after its usefulness. And Drew, he just sat there, as if there were some Rajingiev principle he was adhering to that went against the normal human reflex to leave lovers to quarrel on their own.

Her self-consciousness turned to a shiver. She didn't feel like herself. "If I have to call my husband to pick me up or if I have to call a cab I'm never coming back here—and I want to come back."

"Drew, if you two want to play, I'll go somewhere else," he said, trying to be heroic.

"No man, I lost the desire," Drew said.

A month later, jogging in the woods, she'd think back on

her from going, and she wanted to go. She put her coat back on, locked the front door, got in her Triumph and drove over to Havtha. His truck was there, with a Tibetan-like pillow on the driver's seat, and his car wasn't. Claudia was driving his truck, she realized. She waited on the porch.

He saw her as he drove up and thought about turning around, but he didn't. He walked up the stairs onto the porch and stood there. He seemed taller than ever to her.

"Caleb—I have to talk to you."

"I thought you didn't want to talk," he said.

"I didn't mean forever—I meant I didn't want to talk on that Friday—the day you told me to call you. Had you answered, I would have, though. What I really meant was, I didn't want to talk about the rehearsal either," she said.

"I can't talk right now, I'm very busy. I have to record something and get it out today."

"You're angry. I don't want you to be angry at me," she said.

"I'm not angry, but I've got to go," he said severely.

"It won't take long."

"I can't."

"Is it that you don't want to be friends anymore, is that it?"

"No. I want to be your friend, I'm just busy. I've got to go now."

He opened Havtha's beautiful, old, oak door and walked in.

"Caleb—" she said as he closed the door behind him.

She thought about sitting on the porch, waiting for him, but then thought better of it. She got in her car and looked into the rear view mirror and thought, *Of course. I look terrible. And of course I look terrible, I feel like shit. If I had looked better, he would have had time. There's always time for a neotenous beauty. There was a sweetness in his eyes for the one moment on the stairs before he got a good look at me. Then I saw the anger. But how could I look good now?*

In fact, she had it wrong. He did see her beauty. . . .

⌒

After a few days she called him again, from the bathroom. His voice was venomous.

"Caleb, I won't take up too much of your time."

"Okay."

"I need to talk to you." She sounded desperate.

"What is it?" he asked, detached, automaton-like.

She couldn't tell him.

"I—I just wanted to know—you said you wanted to be friends, but it sure doesn't feel like we are," she said.

"You're right. I think it's for the best if we're not."

"Okay, " she said, shocked, the words sticking.

And they hung up.

She got in the tub, filled it with her tears, and Caleb floated away.

# *writing her story*

To write is a mode of Eros.          *—Roland Barthes*

Compared with music all communication by words is
shameless, words dilute and brutalize; words depersonalize,
words make the uncommon common.
                                        *—Nietzsche*

What we learn from Jung is that you have to let words swim
into your soul.                         *—Charles Olson*

Back to the life of her husband, and of Julian, but not really.
She slept next to her husband still. Loved Julian as always. But
her nerves were raw and most of her was missing. She even cut
her hair. And though her husband was willing to take her back,
she wasn't willing to go back. She could only think of Caleb.

In some ways she knew Caleb was being morally higher,
and certainly stronger, to be tough and sever it without explanation. Maybe it was his way of loving her, she hoped. Free-
ing her of him. Making it easy for her. Or maybe to make her
feel. *Tough love,* as they said at Heliosen.

Or maybe he had consulted the *I Ching* and had drawn number *thirty-three: Tun: Retreat.*

> Retreat is not to be confused with flight. Flight means saving oneself under any circumstances, whereas retreat is a sign of strength. We must be careful not to miss the right moment when we are in full possession of power and position. Then we shall be able to interpret the signs of the time before it is too late . . .

Or maybe, in his Tuesday session with Ted Selby—the guru, the *man*, the big daddy, "God"—he was instructed to end it. Maybe it was some sort of exercise that Ted thought Caleb needed.

It was certainly a conscious shock, so maybe she just had to be patient. Maybe one day he'd present her with what is called the "second conscious shock" and explain everything.

The truth is, he thought after a while she'd figure it out and stop calling. So really, it was her resolution—her determination—her calling and calling, which forced him to be tough, in the end. He had hoped to retreat quietly, to let it fade away. Out of the gray. But as battle, in isolation. Silent. To explain, to talk, would involve truth. And Caleb believed there were many truths, many "I"s. He still loved her. But he hated her, too. And he was also in between, neither loving nor hating.

Anyway, he had decided to change his focus. That was the point. He was tied to something else. If they talked, he would feel. He would be unable to resist. He would become untethered. Her lips would seduce, her language, her desire. And he did not want to be seduced. He did not want to lose. He certainly didn't want "to know" like she did. There *was* nothing to know. And there was too much. There were many realities. Many truths. Not to force it out. To force would invoke her, would pull her through the wormhole, like Alice through the looking glass, or down the rabbit hole. Just to let it quietly seep out of his cerebrum until he forgot. To let go of that universe.

He had forced her into wanting to fade it, too; he wasn't giving her time to love: "If you don't get out of your marriage . . ." The difference is she was a woman. It was part weakness, part kindness. At the end, she wanted to drag it out as a team, in concert, as collaborators. So everyone could feel good, together. Until they were both ready for an end. Until they were numb.

Now that she had made him admit he didn't want her friendship, she still needed to talk. To understand. But it was also practical and social. It was a small town. Their kids were friends. They would undoubtedly see each other at the school, the post office, the bank. She didn't want to feel sick. She had almost transcended—to the sun!—with her soul mate, and to have to stand behind him while waiting to deposit a check, in silence, with a pain in, she wasn't sure where it would be, was too painful—she couldn't let it happen.

So Caleb got her to fight. Not in the way he wanted, though—in his perverse, silent war which was neither practical nor social. No. She would fight against the silence. For their alliance. Because she didn't want an end. The battle she tried to avoid months before, by giving into his sexual impatience, would be fought now. Now she felt. Now she needed him. She should have fought earlier, she realized. She should have listened to her heart. She shouldn't have surrendered her body so soon. (If she hadn't, he would have either gone onto new eggs or pursued her until she could love—the conservative long-term mating strategy.) Because it had worked, her plan. A way to the soul *was* through the body. And Caleb had it now, or part of it—at least she thought he thought so.

She would fight for a happy ending. And if it couldn't be

happy, then she'd settle for peaceful. And if she couldn't get that, then *her* kind of ending, one with meaning.

Besides, she had something to tell him. She went to her computer and reread his last e-mail:

No, your article did not attach. As for replies, you can tell Freddy:

Go ahead, pick from the willowing beauty tree, the fruit is ripe and bountiful. But it only lasts a season.

She clicked reply and wrote:

NOT A PARABLE ABOUT HOW BEAUTY OR LOVE FADE

Today is the last day of the harvest season and a girl is sitting by the river, cold, remembering.

It was an autumn day and the girl had been working in the beauty tree grove very hard, season after season. She sat beneath one of the trees for shade and to rest while she thought about the work ahead of her when suddenly, without warning, the beauty tree dropped a piece of her fruit which fell right beside her. She was stunned by its crimson color, its aroma, how it felt so right in her small hands. And she was hungry. But she had been told never to pick from the beauty tree. Unable to think of work or punishment, she held the fruit firmly. She only wanted the fruit. To have it. To hold it. To smell its heavenly perfume. To behold it. To taste its warm, sweet juice.

But she was afraid to eat it, to put it to her lips and take it into her. But the tree whispered softly, "Go ahead, sweet girl, you have worked very hard and you have suffered and you were meant to eat this fruit."

When the girl had finished eating, she held the core in her hand and carefully removed the beautiful seeds, each so perfect and round. And she held them to her heart and promised herself that she would plant the seeds in a sacred place where she could go to nourish them every day until they were realized.

On the first new moon thereafter, she carried the seeds of the beauty fruit down to the river and planted them.

And now, as she sat by the river on the first day of the new cold season she remembered. And her soul told her all the things she needed to know: that she would never have that fruit again, that she couldn't step into the river twice, that she wasn't who she was yesterday or a second ago. But she had been destined to eat it. It would have dried up, become rotten on the ground, had she not.

Now she shall always have that fruit, the fruit of her labor, as she will return to the river and one day eat the fruit again.

A month passed without response from him. She composed a mensalic e-mail and sent it to him.

Caleb,

In September we met in the school hallway. We talked about Julian and Lily and I tried to resist you. I prayed I'd never run into you again, but I did.

It was in October that your car was blocked and you walked me home—an act that seems like nothing to you—but for most, unheard of. We sat at the table, on the living room floor, on the bench, me on the heater, you on the threshold—stood in the kitchen, too (a place, I found later, which always aroused me when I was with you). And we both knew, though you seemed more certain or determined, that we would be together.

And then that night in November when my house was ours. I made you dinner, you played, and I sang. You almost went back to Heliosen—said you had something to work on that night. Now I wonder if it was Claudia. But you stayed. And we made love, and you told me you loved me.

By the end of December you weren't talking to me. I was writing you. Thinking about you too much, trying to process your sudden withdrawal from my life. Wondering what your initial rush to commit was about. Why you had no patience.

And now it's January. It feels like you'll never be in my life again. And I don't understand why that has to be.

I am sorry if I hurt you. I am sorry I couldn't love you fast enough. Sorry I called you a prick in front of Drew.

You know what I want from this. I'm hoping to understand what happened from your side. Don't want you out of my life. Don't understand why you seem to want me out of yours. You didn't give me much of a chance to be a friend. If we had talked after our fight, something might have shifted. We might have become great friends, or lovers. But you don't seem to want either.

Perhaps I will always have the same questions to you about us, they'll just get buried. And I may always want to have something with you—to be related to you—or rather—relating to you, but that can get buried, too.


Caleb read her words over and over; they swam through him. Then he thought about wormholes. About hyperspace. About other universes. Other realities. Focus. Vision. He closed his eyes and prayed, and then he wrote her. And wrote her.

And then he sent her this:

It's not my intention to be mean, but your needs and questions mean nothing to me. You are an external, an impediment to what I am waiting for: an internal shift; a transcendence. I don't want externals in my life right now, no entanglings. So until this moment of revelation comes, I do not wish to be contacted. Please respect my search, my work.

Best wishes,
Caleb

But this is what he had written first:

I am sorry I have been unable to talk to you. You deserve my respect and consideration. Understand that I have actively intended to give you these since I have known you, though I may not have succeeded fully in each moment.

The truth is, I have felt closer to you in moments than I have to anyone—like you are my very self. What I have seen, and what seems so daunting, is that there is a big part of you that doesn't want that, and even seems to be allergic to it. I felt quite open to you at the rehearsal, but I saw immediately that you were not. When I tried to push through your attitude by engaging you, and you reacted all out of proportion to the situation, the impossibility of any kind of real relationship between us became apparent. I am not blaming you, but I also don't see signs that you see the need to address your psychological baggage.

You know I thought you were the one. But I find it hard to continue to love you without your love. And I don't see that as a possibility. You have my respect and good wishes.

May we see what needs seeing,
C

But of course, she never saw that letter.

So, a week later she wrote and sent him:

I know you want to be left alone by me, but that will
have to wait.

I tried to talk to you in person at Havtha. And tried to
tell you in my parable. Thought about telling you on
the phone many times but couldn't—I was pregnant,
Caleb. And it was yours. I miscarried on Sunday. I don't
like communicating this this way but it doesn't matter
now. It only mattered before.

My last e-mail was an attempt to get you to talk to
me in person and be warmer so I could tell you. Anyway,
I suppose I should be grateful. I know you don't want
advice, so here is no advice: Wisdom—non-attachment—whatever you call it—*with* compassion; honesty
with others and self (had you been truthful with me I
would have trusted you and then maybe loved you and
then everything you wanted from me would have come
so easily). I will leave you alone now.

But she couldn't leave it alone. What she wanted more
than anything was to talk to him, to sing her songs for him.
She could no longer paint. She was drunk on his Dionysian.

His silence forced her to write. And she hated it. It was
logocentrically male. There was so much more. So much more
than written language. It was too far away. Sign . . . and signified. But it was all she had to keep herself from drowning, to
keep herself afloat.

She wrote him letters she would never send and wrote
about love . . .

She wrote:

*1. Evolution*
Ancient, pheromonal, mechanical, automatic, algorithmic, spiritual, instinctual, "reptilian-brain," id, deep, primal, Rajingiev's instinctual center, Kandinsky's "artistry," Kagan's "emotional tone."

*2. Experience*
Old, intermediate, imprinting (parents), later relationships, limbic, ego, Rajingiev's emotional center, Kandinsky's "personality," Kagan's "basic identity."

*3. Culture*
New, superficial, superego, plastic, neocortex, forebrain, Rajingiev's intellectual center, intentional, conscious, Kandinsky's "style," Kagan's "superficial traits."

Sometimes we are not sure why something turns us on or off. Is it from something deep and therefore something to listen to? Or is it something we've learned from the culture and therefore something that is flexible, able to change, less fixed— something maybe to examine critically. When it's from psychological experience (parents or later, others) we also must be critical. And why do I have a bias that the "ancient" information is somehow more valid, more valuable, more important, real? EP theory says there's probably a module for killing which has persisted for eons but that doesn't make it "valuable."

Perhaps in part we learn who we are from what we value. And what we value and how we make that determination ultimately lies beyond evolution, culture and our experience. Though minds have been shaped by an evolutionary process—every choice my ancestors made

reflected in the arrangement of cytosine, adenine, gua-
nine and thymine over and over again (and my ancestors
created culture, and culture influences psychological
relationships, which then alters us physically—ultimately genetically, which affects culture, and the cycle
goes on)—it is the soul, essence, homunculus, the I, the
spirit, mind, that plays with them—allowing culture to
weigh heavily . . . or not, allowing our deep nature to
rule or not, allowing our past to shape our behavior and
feeling or not. We are the sum of those things but more,
we are transcendent, not emergent. We are human; we
have the potential for free will if we wish.

Was it because I didn't trust him that prevented me from
coming? *He* didn't need trust. He wouldn't have to carry a
child for nine months, blah, blah, blah, the whole story.
What he needed was a signal of commitment. He was
looking for weakness. (He would have had me fifteen years
ago.) He was looking for a woman who would give to him,
despite anything. For a woman who loved him so much she
would carry his child and not expect a thing, be a good
mother. And when I wasn't able to do that, he finally used
that back door, to a woman who would. Everything for him
is about survival . . . survival of his genes . . . about strategy,
a seducer's strategy, a cheater's strategy.

He basically has the same battle, the same conflict I
have. I remember once I told him that I thought he
would leave me for the next hot-thing he ran into. And I
was surprised when he said he felt I would leave him for
the next hot-shot *I* ran into. Claudia is plain and probably very nice. She will be a good mother. She will not
leave Caleb. She will put up with him. She will let him
cheat. She will let him leave her and take him back, if he

ever wants to go back. That's what people do when they love.

I am fascinated by what some evolutionary theorists call R-strategists and K-strategists. Cads versus dads. Men whose strategy it is to mate with as many women as possible with little parental investment versus men who mate with few and are high on parental investment. It's a higher type—the K-strategists, evolutionarily, at least. Clams produce hundreds of thousands of eggs and leave. They're R-strategists par excellence. Humans are at the extreme end of the spectrum. But within the human species, we can all be classified as more R or K . . .

And is that who Caleb is? Is he Mr. R? Is his strategy—his mating strategy—who he really is? Is it hard-wired as it may be for some men? Or is he just this way from his early childhood experiences? Or some combination? *Is it* a lost battle and that's just who he is? An R-strategist . . . a cad, not a dad. And that for him to "transcend" he will need to accept his essence—to stop fighting it and embody it?

His work was about observing the energy of the descending octave—the octave of creation—sex energy. To watch mechanical hot love, passionate love—what kept him moving . . . Because what he wanted to do (because of a cultural pressure?) was to practice the evolutionary octave—the intentional conscious kind of love . . . warm love, companionate, committed conscious love. To work at love. To observe the mechanics of passion and transcend it. To be Mr. K.

Maybe Caleb was right about it being beyond evolution. And perhaps Rajingiev's "essence" *is* beyond evolution. And so, even if Caleb is hard-wired to be an R-strategist—perhaps his essence is something else entirely. In watching the many "I"s within the triune layers of evolution, experience and culture, he can find the one true "I"—his essence.

With everything I know, and protecting myself like I did, still, everything practically shunts me toward the alpha male, toward high, high testosterone—toward the R-strategist: my imprinting (my alpha father), my later experiences and relationships with these kind of men, which hardwired some of my feelings, evolution (know I inherited a brain module that finds high testosterone men attractive), and finally culture which seems to be ambivalent about these men, valuing them as the ideal and yet tempering it with a nod to the caring, nurturing, sensitive male. It boils down to this: I am sexually and amorously attracted to these men—insane, difficult, creative, impulsive, megalomaniacal, powerful, jealous, passionate, opportunistic, needy, sexual, controlling, domineering—but know in a deep way and from experience that I must not pair bond with them for long. Not enough to raise a child. They will leave. They will destroy. It is in their nature. They have evolved that way. The testosterone pushes them. The serotonin that surges from being alpha male pushes them—toward the younger, or the more beautiful, or just toward something different.

Am I just proof of the sexy-son hypothesis? Like those female zebra finches who cuckold their hardworking mate with gorgeous male zebra finches, who, it turns out, surprise, surprise, are inattentive fathers. Even at the level of those tiny finches, there are contracts. "I'll

give you my superior genes," says the beautiful male
zebra finch, "you, female cuckolder, you work hard—and
get that mate of yours to help." Yikes.

To love a high testosterone male means to live with a
constant tension. They are jealous and passionate,
*deceivers ever, to one thing constant never.* And to live with
the fear that today they might yell or hit me and tomorrow be gone. And now, the one thing I trusted, my
unhealthy desire for bad boys, seems to be gone. Where
do I turn? Women? Celibacy? Raising Julian on my own
and dating high T men who will bring bursts of bliss
and misery but never be able to bring me happiness?

Do I dare try to love a high testosterone man against
everything my mind and body has learned as defense?
Do I stay with my normal testosterone husband who is
faithful and steady? I don't know if I'm numb or miserable or just miserable because I'm numb.

Our romantic and relationship problems, hence our
problems, because these are the things that matter to us
most, stem from the conflict between 1, 2, and 3. When
my EEA/reptilian/gatherer brain (Evolution #1) turns on
to a dominant male and my forebrain (Culture #3) turns
off or tells me to turn on to a lower T male, I have a conflict. Feelings become congested, tied up, confused, because
I don't know where to invest.

I fear it's all mathematical and it saddens me. Is it, as
Wittgenstein wrote, that "the body is the best picture of
the human soul"?—that, as Nietzsche wrote, "the entire
evolution of the spirit is a question of the body"?

Isn't love more than market value equity exchange?
(She's pretty but not smart, he's rich but unattractive—
they're in love!) More than an assessment of someone's
genes and hormones and brains by their bodies and

actions? And if it's not? What if it's just about ensuring certain modules persist because our ancestors "created" them. What's unromantic about wanting to perpetuate altruism? And what happened to the young woman who believed in love beyond all this shit!?? I want her back. And I want the soul in evolution. I need to be seduced but this onion has too many layers.

# *life's a picnic*

Comfort me with apples
for I am sick with love.
        —*Song of Songs*


Of all the people in the world,
why should I love you?
        —*Kate Bush*

It was April and balmy. Winter seemed like a distant memory.
She could hardly even remember what it was like to feel cold,
though it had just snowed in late March. It was a quarter to
three already and she needed to pick Julian up early to avoid
seeing Caleb. They had an unspoken rule: Julian gets picked
up early, Lily, late. It put the pressure on her, of course.
It was ten minutes to three and the children at school were
playing outside in the yard. Julian ran radiantly to her with
open arms. "Mom!"

"Sweetie!" She bent down and kissed and hugged him.

He pushed on her 'til they were both on the ground—a game he had always liked to play with her. She paid no attention to the looks of the other "early" parents and teachers. Lily came over to join the lovefest. The three of them hugged. She fixed Lily's hair, removing the dangling barrette and fastening it back to one side.

"Hi Dad!" Lily said. "You're early."

*He's early* . . . Her stomach imploded. The second conscious shock.

She stood up and turned around.

"Hi," she said.

"Hi."

"Can I play for a little longer with Lily?" asked Julian.

"I don't know, sweetheart—does Lily have to get going?" she asked in the direction of Caleb.

"No. It's okay."

"Yay!" The two ran off to the playhouse.

She moved her body back to show Caleb he wasn't locked in to talking to her. And he came in toward her. He looked at her intensely.

"How are you?" she asked.

"I'm doing all right."

"I hear you're producing 'Omphalos.'" She was trying to be light.

"Yeah. We're almost done."

"How are you?"

"I'm okay."

She was close enough to him that she could smell him. It didn't matter what they were saying. They were together. But they were in the middle of the schoolyard and so Caleb led her to the side of the school just twenty feet away—

"We should talk. . . ."

They stood there looking at each other. Finally they were

going to talk. He touched her hip. And pulled her into him. And he kissed her right in front of the early parents and the teachers and the kids. Most of them didn't notice. But some did.

"I'd like to take you home right now," he told her.

She leaned into him and kissed him as if to say *I'd like to come home with you right now.* But they had parental duties: "I think we should take the kids on a picnic instead," she said.

"You're right, okay."

They walked over to the playhouse. Julian and Lily's teachers were watching and incredulous. They couldn't wait until every last child was gone so they could wildly replay together what they had just witnessed. Why were they so excited? Was it the rush of seeing an illicit act made explicit? Is it that they fantasized about such things? Whatever it was it made them giddy. Maybe they were just happy for them.

"Hey kids, wanna go for a picnic?"

"Yeah," shouted Lily.

"Me too!" Julian shouted even louder.

And they were off to the farm stand in Caleb's beat up old truck as if this were the most natural thing in the world.

"I'm sorry about the miscar—"

"It's okay," she said quietly, sweetly.

"I've thought about it a lot," he told her.

"Me too."

"I worried it was somehow my e-mail to you that—"

"Oh, no. No. I think it was teratogenic. My floors were sanded and the dust was really toxic. I don't think the fetus—it wasn't even a fetus—was established enough as a being to take it."

He took her hand and let her see his tears.

"So, what happened, Caleb? Why wouldn't you talk to me?"

"It's complicated. I'm not sure I know really. There'll be time to talk about it later."

"Was it the rehearsal?"

"Well, sweetie, that didn't help. I suppose I told myself that if you left, we were over. I wasn't going to invest in you anymore. You weren't worth it. Because your leaving showed me you weren't committed."

"I *left* because I couldn't be treated like that. Maybe if we had been alone I might have been able to argue with you. But it was awkward with Drew there. It's one thing to be yelled at and called a cunt, it's another when someone is there to witness it. I guess I was hoping to talk to you in the car that night or on the phone—if I had known that was my last chance— "

"It wasn't. I'm here. And don't fuck it up, okay?"

"Okay, Caleb, I won't fuck it up," she laughed. "You know, years ago, many years ago, I would have stayed that last night— at the 'rehearsal.' I would have been so turned on by your anger and hostility that as soon as Drew left, or even before he left, while he was there, if I could have managed it, that's how perverse I was, I would have wanted to give you every- thing I could—sexually. And back then, would have—despite any ambivalence you had. But by myself, without therapy, Rajingiev, self-help books, without any real help, I broke that pattern. When you yelled at me, I felt nothing. I felt cold. I wanted to flee. And that's a pretty healthy response to some- one who's treating you badly. What's strange is that I missed that unhealthy feeling that night. Part of me wanted to be turned on by your anger. I wanted to want to stay. My body didn't let me."

They sat there eating dried figs and stuffed grape leaves, goat cheese and bread. He finally asked, "What's going on with you and—?"

"I might ask you the same thing," she said.

"Claudia? There was never much going on—you know that. We're friends, that's about it."

"About it?" she queried.

"It," he assured her. "So answer my question," he prodded.

"We're over. We've been over—you had to know that. He stays at the house once or twice a week and sleeps downstairs on the couch. He's looking for his own place. He's been staying in the city most nights, though."

"I think it's more like he's here four times a week, if you count weekends. I used to drive by the house. Saw his car there. I saw you doing yoga one morning," he smiled at her.

"I can't believe you!" she laughed.

"I fantasized about opening your door and walking over to you on the floor, taking that leotard off you and—"

"Oh, Caleb," she said warmly, "I was probably thinking about you, *too*. . . . That's what I used to do: think about you—with my hair down and wet and jasminy, listening to *Om*—imagining you on me, with every *Om*, you going into me. . . ."

"I want to be inside you again," he said.

"Then come tonight. And stay. Can you come?" she asked.

"I am not leaving you until you tell me to," he said.


The children were picking wildflowers and greenery and Julian had fashioned them into a bouquet. He handed it to Lily and said, "Lilibel Matthews, will you marry me?"

She took his hand and said, "Yes, I will marry you Julian Trimber."

Julian then pulled her toward the couple lying out in the grass. Caleb couldn't help but notice the physical beauty in everything he looked at. Lily's golden hair bounced shafts of light back to the sun as she bounded toward him with Julian. His beloved beside him, gazing at him with large doe eyes which made him happy to be alive.

"Dad, Julian and I want to get married. Will you marry us together?"

They looked into each other's eyes more seriously than either thought was possible. They felt lifted by the pull of fate. They were like birds riding air currents. They gave in to their children's magic and to their own magic, and to something beyond them.

"C'mon, Caleb, marry us!" Julian shouted.

The four of them ran over to an apple tree. Some of its blossoms had fallen and created a pink carpet where Caleb performed the ceremony. The children danced around the tree and as they circled it, Caleb pulled her off to the side.

"I love you," he said, solemnly.

"I love you," she said exuberantly.

"I want to do what they did. Will you do that with me?"

"I will."

They kissed. And then the four of them danced around the tree, singing and forgetting everything which came before and not knowing anything which was to come soon after.

⁓

She chose love. And though she didn't know how long it would last or when he'd leave, she'd love. But it wouldn't be a "Love Stories" ending after all. She would not go to Heliosen and be buoyed by the community. Neither of them wanted it. Caleb was especially ready to make a break. And so, with her husband living in the next town, Caleb and Lily moved in to her house.

A man and a woman together is romantic; a man and his daughter with a woman and her son is something else—even if the kids aren't there Tuesdays and Thursdays and every other weekend. There were many difficult adjustments: Lily getting used to a new home, her soon-to-be-step-mom and step-brother; Julian, getting used to sharing his home, his mom, and all the permutations that come when you weave two families together to form one. The back and forth movement from household to household. It was hard for Caleb and it was hard for her, too. They were tested each day.

But they were in love. And they made love whenever they could.

One day in August, when Julian and Lily were off at summer camp, Caleb was in the attic putting the last touches on the rooms he had made for the children. She was downstairs making a chicken for him, the one he called "sex chicken" because the first night she made it they thought it might have come close. She had made some sun tea from the mint that grew in abundance out their back door and refrigerated it. When it was cold enough she went to the freezer and lovingly put three ice cubes in it. Before she went up, she went back out to get a few leaves and placed them in the glass.

She climbed the stairs to the attic carrying the iced tea.

"Sweetie, how'd you know?" he asked.

"I just did." She handed him the tall glass.

"Thanks," he said in that voice that was enough to warm her below. He removed the leaves and held them tight in his hand, drank the elixir and put the empty glass down as she stood watching him. "Mmmmmmm." After a brief kind of prayer, or reflection, he ate the leaves. Then, without a word, he put his hand on her hip and lower back and led her to a futon on the floor by the window. The sun was coming in and they felt blessed. He undressed her, and then himself. He was inside her almost immediately, their eyes open, taking each other in, their bodies fused, indistinguishable from one another.

"I want to make a baby with you," he said. "It's what god wants."

She opened her legs wider and pressed him in deeper with her arms.

"And when our child is born, do you know what I'll tell him?" he whispered.

"What?" she whispered back.

"He was born from love."

# *Epilogue*

Would any link at all be missing in the chain of art and science if woman, if the works of women were missing? . . . Woman attains perfection in everything that is not a work: in letters, in memoirs, even in the most delicate handiwork, in short in everything that is not a *métier*—precisely because in these things she perfects herself, because she here obeys the only artistic impulse she has—she wants to please. . . . Only in this century has woman ventured to turn to literature: . . . she dabbles in writing, she dabbles in art, she is losing her instincts. But *why?* if one may ask?        *—Nietzsche*

When they heard far over the sea singing so enchantingly sweet that it drove out all other thoughts except a desperate longing to hear more, and they turned the ship to the shore where the Siren's were at, Orpheus snatched up his lyre and played a tune so clear and ringing that it drowned the sound of those lovely fatal voices.        *—Homer*

*the end*

We have art lest we perish from the truth.
—Nietzsche

Then she wrote: *Caleb, The story has an ending now. It's not perfect but at least it's complete.* And sent him "Siren's Song" as an e-mail attachment.

Caleb resisted reading the story for several weeks. But he couldn't just delete that huge file. He finally read it.

He hated it. He had to. *But he thought it was well written in parts. Maybe it was too close.*

He clicked reply and wrote: *I read your story. I was not seduced. Not this time. It's a man's world, maybe you should try broadcasting. Good Luck, Caleb*

Come on, you had to suspect this. The eternal recurrence of the story. Story after story after story. But now, finally, here's the end. Oh, but remember the law of no return, of the octave, of the triadic dialectic—from synthesis to thesis?

It may be just the beginning.

So, in a way, the story doesn't end for her when you finish this. And it won't end for you either. It's been sticking, this story, this memesome. Myelin. It's fast. Axons. Dendrites. You've been living it. You've taken it into you. You've digested it, assimilated it, incorporated it. You'll use it, plagiarize and betray it, I know. I can handle it. You're gonna say things to your friends and think it's you. And it might be. But it's probably these memes. Yep, it's in your synapses. It's in all your layers. Maybe not all of them. Maybe not those deep ones . . .

Please don't think I'm being arrogant. This isn't really mine. These memes are not mine. They don't belong to me. Not really. I can't really lay claim to anything. And anyway, *everything* you read, look at, hear, feel, adds to you. This book is no different than anything else you come into contact with, in that way. That reading the arrangement of these fifty thousand words does something to your brain chemistry, that it alters it in some way, for a few hours certainly, and perhaps longer isn't saying that much. (Anyway, you don't really care about this. Why should you? It's just a bunch of words. You can't fuck them; they can't listen to your hopes and dreams; and they can't buy you a nice dinner at Balthazar.)

What I'm trying to say is that I understand that the effect this has on you is not related to the merit or quality of this work. I am not trying to toot my horn when I say you are and will be affected; I am stating a fact of nature. But maybe all that's sort of folly. I know this is mine. I was just protecting myself. An elaborate defense. Because I know you've edited it some—rejected it. That's good, though. I'm the parent who must love you though you have decided to become something other than I wished for. I respect what you do with this meme—this memesome. And I hope you did more with it than I did. Want you to *do* more with it than I did. Isn't that what every parent wants for their child?

You know you created something, in your reading of this. You must know you've been the artist all along. . . . How could it be any other way? You can't get into my head . . . not that I don't want you to. I've been trying. But I know I can't be known. Your reading . . . is your reading.

The truth is, what I really want to know is . . . are you a great artist? Would I feel joy at your admiration? Has bliss been created? A dialectics of desire? But that's the slut in me.

I mean, doesn't it mean *something* that you have found this book, that you have made it to this strange epilogue? Ah, the fate card . . . But also, you didn't put it down after you read all that crap about communist moles. You must have seen something. That means something to me. . . .

Look, there's something I want you to understand about this book, this memesome, this synthesis. I tried explaining it before. It's become thesis, a shock point. I sound arrogant again. It's not about me, though. It's about you. This book is a shock point. It's Julian in the night, waking you up. What do you do? Do you go back to sleep?

In case you're confused, only that last chapter, "life's a picnic," the one that seems biblical and sappy, is fiction. There are parts of you that will keep that ending and forget all this nonsense here. That's fine. You're the artist, you can do what you want with this. Because these words belong to you now. Every single one.

So let me tell you why she wrote "life's a picnic." You can probably figure it out: she wrote it to hold onto sanity. Because like her need for her dreams to have an end, she needed the story to have one, too. Caleb would have called it *closure*. She really hated that word. She wasn't crazy about *engorged* either.

Anyway, she just couldn't end with *She got in the tub, filled it with her tears, and Caleb floated away.* What kind of ending was that?

In the end, "life's a picnic" was a way to heal. It was another reality—a parallel universe. Another story.

But it was also poetry. A song. A prayer. A conscious shock. It was an ending stuck on as clear and eternal as black and white.

Now, the rest of the story in "Siren's Song" was true, at least, according to the way she saw it. She wrote it down to show him how she remembered, because he believed her forgetting was a sign. It was a way to prove it had been there. In the gray. Memory. Love. Desire. It had been there—had always been there—as *certain* and *imperceptible* as ovulation had been there.

And she wrote it down because she didn't want to lose it. From the gray, to black and white.

To find and create meaning.

But back to the real story:

She sat there looking at those sharp words on the screen, *I was not seduced. Not this time. It's a man's world, maybe you should try broadcasting*, with a shadow version of anger and sadness. From her window she could see the bare ficus in the backyard. She had known it was tropical, that it would never have survived the winter, that it would never have come back in the spring, it couldn't. It was poetry what she had told him. She thought language and desire could change him, could change things, rearrange them. But the tree, spindly and ashy, wasn't metaphysical, it was ontic, real, earthy; it was the damn truth. And it was dead.

Then she remembered back to that first day at her house when he told her the future lay in rest, as potential, until it was awakened by our choices. How reality was already created but that we chose our fate by where we placed our focus in the form of thought, feeling, emotion, and prayer. She had tried with the ficus.

And then the revelation: that her stories were a form of thought, feeling, emotion, and prayer. They were shadow versions of reality. And how she focused the only way she knew how. On one man.

He was right, she could see. She needed to focus elsewhere. On the many. To go against her estrogenic impulse. To amplify the beautiful risk-taking, ovum-seeking testosterone that most every woman has running through her body. It wasn't a political act. Women had fought and won the battle to broadcast already. It was a conscious act against her nature. It felt as if it were by default, but it wasn't. It had been what she wanted all along.

She began "Love Stories" with a desire. A desire she could not admit to herself. Caleb answered her desire: her desire for love and her desire for story. Now she would bring their love story into discourse, into a social act, beyond man and woman. Into a man's world. It would become more. Perhaps art. And it would save her life.

# Third Force

Jesus said, 'What I say, I say unto you all: watch.' And it would be wise to listen. Watch. Don't push. See your habit, pattern— penetrate it with seeing and accept it, don't judge it. This is the way toward breaking patterns, toward freedom.

—*Edward Rolby*

# BABY THEORY

That's what Helen sent to Ed Rolby. That whole thing. *Conscious Shock.*

And he read it with pleasure and something like love . . . maybe because he'd already met her.

I know. I told you it was over. And it was. But then I got to thinking you sort of liked the repetition, the pattern, the cycle. The eternal recurrence. Like I said before, I'm a slut. I want to please; it gives me pleasure. But not only that. I'm not just some pleasuring logos-pusher, feeding this quasi-metafiction habit I've possibly hooked you on. No. I'm co-dependent and a selfish addict. See, in some way this story I'm about to tell you was born from my compulsion to explain what I meant by it "not ending." About how it doesn't *end* for her. How *Conscious Shock* was the beginning for her. But after "Baby Theory," I promise, you're on your own. I don't want to be an enabler, after all. Though you probably can't wait for it to end. The story after story after story after story . . . So, stop . . . if you want. But I think this one's pretty good. And it's true, too. And it really is the end. Our *petit morte.* (Was it good for you? It was good for me.)

Our rebirth.


Oh. One more thing: see how the slut is warm love and the addict is hot love? And see how they both have elements of selflessness and selfishness in them?

(Sorry. It's hard to stop.)

# *harvesting*

It was July in Hundton. Helen was driving her old, red Volvo to her organic CSA farm, though she usually rode her bike with the pretty wicker basket.

*When the world ends collect your things, you're comin' with me . . . when the world ends . . .*

She was listening to Dave Matthews and thinking how happy she was she no longer lived in dirty old Park Slope. She was thinking about Evan—the inspiration for Caleb, the man Caleb was based on—having just seen him at the post office.

It was the first time her heart didn't race when she ran into him; the first time her face stayed cool. Her body had made peace with him, and so had she. She knew she had Time to thank for that. But still, where did the pain go? The pain of unresolution. The pain of not getting to say all that she needed to say. The pain of losing him just like that. Was it in her thighs? Was it in *Conscious Shock?* Was it in her kids?

*I'm gonna rock you like a baby in a carriage car . . .*

She was thinking about her kids. They were with their dad for the month in Cape Cod, and she loved the freedom, but she missed them, too. She was smiling at the children on scooters and skateboards as she drove by with her windows down. She was smiling at the mountains. She was looking forward to summer squash.

At the farm, she and Scott Tunich, the owner, talked a lot as she filled three small bags. Somehow they got to talking about "the will," of all things, about the many "I"s. Scott was saying he just wanted to be integrated—one "I." It was fun for Helen to talk to this environmental science professor/innovative farmer about "the will" as she gathered her fruits and vegetables. She quoted Leibniz and took a bite of a mustard green.

"Elise made a lovely dinner, Helen. And for dessert, there's a rhubarb, squash, cinnamon thing. You have to try it. Come on . . . We'll put all this stuff in the big fridge. . . ."

And they walked over to the farmhouse and into the dining room.

"Nobody is what they seem to be," Ed was saying in his husky, slight Welsh accent, to a tableful of very attractive, enlightened farm workers and students, when Helen and Scott walked in. He held up a lit candle.

"Only those who have burned away the dross of what they *aren't* are free to appear however they wish. To see essence is a rare event. The sun is ever eclipsed by the moon . . . And who is this *bella luna*?" Ed said, looking at Helen standing there with Scott.

Ordinarily Helen would have had some fairly witty response, but not with Ed. He was an imposing figure. First of all, he was enormous—about six-foot-four and quite mesomorphic. And he was very handsome. But there was something about the pipe and his straw hat—at the table—that made him simply intimidating.

"This is Helen, Ed. Please don't embarrass her or she won't come back," Scott said smiling.

"Hello, everyone . . . Elise, Ed—" she said.

They all said hello in their various ways and Ed said,

"Ah, Helen. Please come and sit and have some *saag paneer*. . . ."

And he pulled a chair from the wall, putting it between the young woman who was sitting next to him and himself, so that Helen could sit there. Helen sat down feeling weak, breathless. She had put two and two together: the talk about essence, the accent. This was Edward Rolby, she realized, the founder and guru of Solaren—the real community which she had based Heliosen on.

"We were just talking about another sense of the word *respect*. The conventional definition involves a kind of deferential submission, but etymologically it connotes something more dispassionate—re-spect: to look again. We were saying that it's lazy, really, to be satisfied with a preconception of someone and leave it at that. To truly respect someone means to look again, every moment. To keep seeing where someone is, both in terms of their strengths and weaknesses. So you know what you can expect from them, what they are capable of. Then you don't get let down or surprised, because you see them as they are in a cool light. And you see that you have the same weaknesses, or perhaps different but equal ones. And by this you are freed of the master/slave, dominant/submissive power game, in which everyone is measured as either better or worse than our idea of ourselves—a dreadful condition."

He looked at her, demanding with his eyes and body: "And your thoughts on this?"

Helen got her breath back. She felt like a schoolgirl. She took a sip of wine that a young, goateed, angel-faced farm worker poured her, and said dutifully, "Yes, that's lovely. Of course. Yes, I agree . . . to respect someone in this way, to be open to their potential, to recognize and respect their ever-changing states, to see that much of what they are is not their 'essence,' and accept them, is not as selfless as it seems. It's a gift actually, to oneself, to re-spect others this way . . . it's a kind of social flexibility that helps one to be of good cheer . . ."

"Yes, yes, that's right," Ed said.

"Like, if I stick with the belief that, at bottom, my department chair is a misogynist piece of shit," she continued, "what does that do for me? It just makes me react in certain ways to him that continues the process of shit. But when I'm open to the possibility of seeing more than that, then things can happen. He can be more than, or better than, a misogynist shit . . . maybe . . . *himself*." Her head was spinning; she didn't even know what she had said. But it wasn't the wine, it was Ed. He took her hand and kissed it. She wanted to run.

*Get me away from this charismatic Gulliver-sage*, the protective part of her was screaming inside. But the fearless part of her, the part that wanted more life—wanted to *stay*, wanted to know this man, this alpha male, this brilliant, passionate man, whom she had only heard of—and written about, calling him Ted. And then there was Evan. Part of her loved the connection with Evan (the real Caleb). But another part was so afraid. She didn't want to think about Evan; didn't want to be reminded. She didn't really trust the peace she thought she had found at the post office earlier that day.

"Beauty *and* brains, a lethal combination," Ed said, giving her a wink.

They talked for a long while as the farm workers and students excused themselves, as Scott and Elise went about clearing the spinachy, squash dishes, as the evening daylight turned into night.

Helen couldn't help but feel there was a reason she was meeting Ed. Yeah, yeah, she knew that was silly and goofy and when people talked that way, she almost stopped listening. But she still couldn't help but think it.

Maybe, since he was the publisher of *Saura Press*—a non-fiction press which dealt with Guerttiev literature and related esoterica—he might know where she could publish *Conscious Shock*, she thought. And yet, to reveal it had anything to do with Guerttiev was tricky. He'd be intrigued. She wasn't sure she wanted that.

"Elise, your *raita* is exceptional!" Ed yelled toward the kitchen.

"Thanks!" Elise yelled back.

"You were talking about essence before," Helen said, feeling half-bold, half-abashed. "I'm very interested in 'essence' . . . I've just written a—I guess a novel that explores it some."

"Really? That's unusual . . . and delightful . . . Essence . . . I'd like to hear more."

"Well, it's about a lot of things. . . . Probably too many . . . love, art, writing, the will, the unconscious . . . it's endless, really, what it's about."

"What's it called?" he asked.

"Ah. *Conscious Shock*," she said, hesitantly.

"Conscious Shock? Conscious Shock! You know the work of Orenne Guerttiev?"

"Just a little. A very, very little," she said.

"Christ! Guerttiev? Where did you come from? I want to read it!" he said, pounding his fist on the table for emphasis, and the wood actually cracked. It was a pretty good crack, too. About a foot and a half long, right down the center of the farm table. Scott and Elise ran in from the kitchen. They were all stunned. Elise started laughing. Then Scott and Helen chortled some, but Ed was silent. He looked like he was praying.

"Come, have some wine," he said to Elise and Scott still standing in the dining room looking like they wanted to get back to the dishes. He poured the wine for them all and lifted his glass and said, "A toast . . . done with attention . . . can change the quality of what is in your glass. . . . You can change its vibrations . . . make it a medicine . . . to life. *Zhivio, l'echaim, bkra shis!*" Then an Arabic prayer. And, "To cracks, to holes, to the places where light can get in. To openings and beginnings! To change!"

The four of them sat there at the newly cracked table smiling and drinking.

"When I was a kid, maybe seven, the same thing happened to this very large friend of my parents—Samuel Cole," Helen said, hoping Ed would forget all about her and Guerttiev. One day she could call him, she thought, and ask him where to send the manuscript. But tonight he was too excited. He'd get into it all hot and heavy. And she just couldn't.

"Samuel Cole? The poet?" said Elise.

"Yeah, that's him. He's been dead for at least thirty years now, but I still remember him well."

"What about Guerttiev, Helen—who cares about poetry?" Ed said. No one knew if he was being ironic.

"Ahm—" Helen said.

"Let her tell her story, Ed!" Elise said.

Ed took a deep breath. "All right, but before I leave to-night, I want to hear about the book," he said.

"Okay, Ed . . ." said Elise, irritated with his insistence.

"So what happened with Cole?" asked Scott.

Ed was smoking a cigarette now and watching Helen.

"Well, he was over for dinner, and he was all excited about something and he pounded on the table—except ours was glass—and it broke into like a thousand pieces. It scared the shit out of me! To this day, I hate glass tables," she told them.

"You seem to have an interesting affect on large men," said Elise smiling.

"I guess. Well, this thing when I was a kid is a well-docu-mented incident.

It's discussed at length in a biography on Cole. According to the book, my dad said that Cole called him that night after the table incident to apologize and tell him that he was his dearest friend. But someone else told the biographer that Cole had characterized the night quite differently . . . that Cole said something like, 'I walked into his house and he started giving me the party line, so I said to him, *Where's your fucking work, boy*, and slammed down my fist and broke his fucking table!'"

Scott and Elise chuckled; Ed was quiet.

Elise said, "What is it about artistic geniuses? Why do we forgive them for breaking tables, and for being sentimental in one moment—cruel in the next?" She smiled at Ed and pat-ted him on his huge shoulder. Ed was mildly interested in this question, as it seemed to pertain to him, but it was Helen's eyes that he was mostly interested in. He couldn't stop watch-ing her.

"That's what we do when we value anything, right?" said Helen. "We pay a price. We're willing to put up with the extreme negatives of artistic geniuses because we need the extreme good they provide. And I don't think you can separate the extremes, that's key. I don't think you get artistic genius without problems . . . don't think you get a visionary without some darkness. It's the nature of the extreme beast. And maybe it has something to do with love."

Scott saw the way Ed was looking at Helen. "I'm going to go finish those dishes," he said, and got up from the table with Elise following.

"Your eyes seem to love everything you look at," Ed said. "Do you love everything you look at?"

"I don't really understand love. . . . No, I don't think I do love everything I look at. I do know that I have very large pupils which make my eyes appear dilated . . . and when people are in love, you know, their eyes dilate. Guess it just looks like I'm in love."

"That's clever. But too reductionist. I say your eyes—with your big pupils—reveal your nature, your essence. Your eyes let more light in—the energy from the sun—they're more receptive. They're naturally loving."

She liked this explanation. She liked that he could turn her analysis on its head. Back to its beginning. Back to mystery.

They talked for awhile like that until Ed said, "I think we should get out of here . . . come . . . we can go to my yurt and drink maté."

Helen's face flushed. She had heard about his yurt, wondered what went on in the yurt. For a little while, she had almost forgotten about him and Solaren, and his connection with Evan.

"Oh, I can't, I have to get home to do a little work before I go to sleep. But I really enjoyed talking with you, Ed."

"All right. But, Helen, I want to see you again. And I want to read *Conscious Shock*. . . . No, I *have* to read it. . . . How about this: Send me the manuscript, I'll read it and we'll meet afterwards. And we can talk about it. How's that?"

"Um, well . . . I'm not quite ready to show it just yet," she said.

"Helen, I don't believe that. Please send it to me. I may know where you can publish it." And he took a pen and sexy matchbook from his linen jacket and wrote: *Edward Rolby, Solaren, 55 Hingett Road.*

"Okay, Ed. I'll send it," she said, putting the obscene matchbook in her purse.

And they went into the kitchen to thank their hosts, who were putting away dishes, and walked out into the star-crisp, hay-drenched Hundton air.

*Rolby! Great!* she said to herself, and she waved goodbye to him from her "personality" and not her essence and got into her Volvo.

She was afraid.

It was so close.

He would surely recognize Caleb. But, maybe not, she hoped, turning on the ignition. Maybe not.

Evan.

Evan . . .

She pressed play:

*When the world ends, collect your things, your comin' with me; when the world ends, you tuckle up yourself with me, watch it as the stars disappear to nothing; the day the world is over, we'll be lying in bed; I'm gonna rock you like a baby when the cities fall . . .*

But then, so what? So much was fiction it didn't matter.

*Well, one thing's for sure,* she told herself, *this is no siren's song . . . I want to publish my art. I'm not looking for love.* And she believed that. (It's the *Mother Nature* meme again—she had to believe it or she would never have sent it to him.)

# sophisticated hookers

Bait the hook well, this fish will bite.    —*Shakespeare*

They met at Tao Bar and sat in the back. It was dark and plush and they ate sushi and drank cognacs.

"I loved it, Helen . . . I was nourished by its thoughtfulness, the entertainment of ideas, the concept-play, the memes, the sex. But the motive behind the last story, I thought was . . . well . . . rather slithery."

"Slithery? What do you mean slithery?" she said.

"I mean, it slithers around your story like the biblical snake . . . it whispers for you to eat the apple, which you do. You keep eating it, keep reveling in the pain, the pleasure, the dramatic revulsion—the delight of the fantasy, until you're nauseated or have indigestion, or both. That's the real siren's song for you, isn't it? . . . You're using me to keep the wormy corpse of the bloody event animated for yourself!"

This wasn't at all what Helen was expecting. She thought they'd have a nice drink. She thought he'd say he liked it and they could talk about essence or something.

She felt agitated, defensive, a little turned on.

"If you remember correctly, I didn't want you to read it—and for this *reason*. But you wanted to, and I thought you might be helpful in finding a publisher. I'm not trying to keep the corpse alive; it's buried. When I sent it, I honestly thought there was a chance . . ."

"That I wouldn't recognize him? Come off it, Helen! There's only one Evan Mckee . . . I mean, who else would say, 'It's a man's world. Maybe you should try broadcasting'? That was classic Evan."

"Actually, *I* wrote that. He never said that. That event never transpired."

"That wasn't Evan? It sure sounded like his virile tongue."

"Yeah, well . . . it was my tongue. What I wrote was fiction. And Evan Mckee is fiction, too . . . in many ways—covered with masks and 'false personality' and 'dross,' as you say. As for your snake metaphor, the part about seduction . . . Yes, of course I want the reader to bite the apple; to take it in. But my goodness—what do you think my intentions *are?* Your final reaction is basically the right one, though—not to be seduced. I write about that some, I think. It's anti-seduction, and it's nauseating. If I really wanted to seduce, I wouldn't put it out there the way I do. That's the point. I'm exploring seduction, not seducing."

"My point was, I'm not so sure I wasn't wanting to be

seduced. And don't be so sure that I haven't been. . . . You know, he talked about you once. He loved you."

She sipped on her cognac. She was pouting.

"Helen, don't get me wrong. I loved it. It was very good for me to read. It showed me things that are useful to see. Evan and I are similar in certain ways. . . ."

And at that he took out some tobacco and started rolling a cigarette.

"I'm glad it was useful for you," she said.

"I'm glad it was useful for *you,*" he said.

"What is that supposed to mean?" she said.

"I'm just reflecting. Whatever it means to you," he said.

"Jesus. I need some more cognac. Can you get me another one, please?"

Ed went over to the bar and got her another. He got himself a double.

"You know what the real problem with it is, though?" he said, handing her the ambery liquid.

"What?" she asked.

"It's anti-transcendent. I mean, what's missing from the story is the underscoring of the repetitious pattern of all the relationships. There's something you can teach here," he said.

"How much more underscoring can I do? I fight very hard with myself as a writer not to be too didactic. To leave gaps. Not to answer *everything*. Not to tie every piece up. Because what I've learned about art, and also love, is that you can't force it. If you really want to teach something to somebody you can't put it in their face. You have to be artful."

"You mean manipulative?"

"No, I mean selfless and loving. I have a need to teach but I've found that my in-your-face style doesn't always help—or teach. That I have to give up my need to want to teach and 'help' sometimes, because I see that's what's needed . . . it's something a mother learns along the way, I think . . . and that when I do that—give up what I hold onto as my identity—"

"And your hook—"

"My *hook*?"

"Yes, your hook."

"Okay, give up my *hook*—then something can really happen for another. And somehow, I am better for it, too. Freed in some way."

"That's quite good . . . quite good. You know, I don't even see the color in your eyes—they're green, right?"

"Yes, sometimes green, sometimes blue."

"Well right now you're one big pupil and you're gorgeous," he said.

"You're sweet to say. Must be the low light."

"Yes. Must be," he said, knowing not to pursue it further.

"I have a confession," he said.

"Oh, *great*, what? What is it?" she said, reaching for a dumpling with her chopsticks.

"I said Evan and I were similar in some ways. . . . What I was thinking when I said that was . . . I had this vague almost preconscious intention of seducing you through this whole reading-your-book process. . . ."

"I see," she said, "until now, I didn't see the similarity at all."

"Yes. One of our hooks is our esoteric knowledge. But, without consideration, such useful and good ideas can be prostituted for weaknesses. I mean, look at Evan: for a little while anyway, he's quite impressive. But ultimately, as you undoubtedly know, he's unable to fully integrate his ideals into his being, even though he's one smart motherfucker. I'd like to think we're different. That my will is stronger; that I have more self-knowledge."

"Hmmm," she said, a bit confused. She wasn't sure if he was "derogating his rival" as they say in evolutionary psychology, or just being honest, or both.

"Anyway, when it became clear that Evan had gotten to you first—and it was pretty early on in the reading—I got sick to my stomach . . . sick with some kind of distorted jealousy; and sick from seeing the truth of what it was I was hoping to do. And then almost heartsick watching it all play out."

A part of her was loving this. The attention. The talk about Evan.

Evan.

Evan.

She wanted to talk more about Evan. But another part didn't care at all; it said, *Ed's the man*. But still another part was upset at herself for wanting to talk more about Evan. Maybe Ed was right about the wormy corpse. How buried could it be if she felt excited talking about this? So, she willed herself away from Evan thoughts. The super "I" won.

"How seductively anti-seductive of you to say . . . I appreciate you telling me, Ed."

"You're a hooker, too, you know," he said.

"Yeah, I guess I *am* a hooker . . . the *stories*, but I'd like to think my self-awareness—my attention to it—negates it. Destroys it. Is anti-seduction."

"It's all seduction. Anti-seduction, seduction. Doesn't matter. One of your hooks (and you have many, as you know) is getting at truths and transmitting them. The baby theories. And of course it doesn't feel that way to you. It feels like that's who you are. And it is, to some degree. And it's the same thing that hooks you. A man who's interested in getting at truths and transmitting them," he said.

"Yeah. I think you're right on that one. I go on about the alpha-thing in *Conscious Shock*, but that's not the hook for *me*. Not really. It's more about what you're talking about— it's a connection based on this similar truth seeking—or, this similar hooking style—if you want to call it that."

"Yes. And it's cyclical, really. You hook by making others use their hooks which hook you. And it goes round and round."

"Until it stops," she said.

"Well, 'the work' is actually interested in getting beyond the hooks. So yes. That's actually the goal. Real love is beyond all these hooks—sexual, emotional, intellectual."

"Ohww! But I like the merry-go-round. I like being hooked."

"But it's ersatz, ultimately. The only thing that is worth anything is attention and action. What we need to find, need to *be,* is 'love-bliss-itself.'"

"And I suppose if I can find love-bliss-itself, I probably don't need hooks," she said, and got up to go to the bathroom.

Ed watched her. Watched her all the way to the back of the bar. Her long auburn hair. Her long, long legs beneath her hand-sewn, cotton red dress. Helen the hooker. Helen the homemaker.

She went into the one stall that was available and looked at the wetness on the seat. It had dirt on it, too, as if someone didn't want to sit on the mess and stood up on the seat. She expected this sort of thing at Port Authority, but Tao Bar? In Hundton? She wiped it with the toilet paper and sat down. *Helen. Helen. It's still you. You've been peeing in bathroom bars for decades and it's still you,* she said to herself, feeling the warm flow of her cognacy urine release, without her intention, feeling young, feeling herself. As she left the otherwise exceedingly clean quarters, she took a long look at herself in the mirror. She looked better than usual, she thought. She thought she looked pretty. And she wondered if it was some kind of affect Ed was having on her that actually changed her features: her eyes wide open, her skin glowing. Or was it just that he made her feel good and so her perception was altered? Or maybe both. Whatever the answer, she was pleased; she could feel good walking back out through the crowd. (So what, she was a good decade older than the average woman there?) She knew the pleasure would end one day; gazing at her reflection; men's gaze. (Probably even by tomorrow, what with the late night and drinking.) But there was no point in denying the pleasure of it now. She took it all in.

"Hello, beauty," Ed said when she returned to the table.

"You sure don't hold back, do you?"

"I try to say no more and no less than what I mean. And what I see is needed. Not as easy as it seems . . . You're a little mercurial, *aren't* you?"

"Mercurial? Where do you get *that* from? And did you eat my last *ebi shu mai?*" she said smiling.

"I did. Sorry. Would you like some more?"

"No, no, I was done . . . just having fun with you . . . Mercurial? I'd like to think I'm more Venusian. Mercurial seems like a masculine trait . . . I think if anything, I have more of a strange passive-receptive quality, almost old-fashioned—but I'm seldom allowed to express it. . . . Actually, can I try that—?" she said, pointing to his last piece of dragon roll.

"Of course," he said, picking up his chopsticks and placing the eel and avocado bundle onto her wooden serving plate.

"You know, I don't see your mercurialness as masculine, by the way. It's part of what makes you beautiful—your quickness, your many-frames-per-second perception. It's one of your feminine charms, actually . . . and I've already seen tonight that if I allow myself to become still, I can feel myself being invited into your finer ways of seeing."

"Ed, that's lovely of you to say," she said. She felt mesmerized by his openness to her, turned on by his self-knowledge and attempts to get at some kind of truth, not necessarily her body. Or not *just* her body.

"As for the receptive trait—you distort it to make it palatable to others; make it contemporary in an age that doesn't respect receptivity."

She had an understanding of this, but she loved the way he said it. The way he made it fact.

"I see, master," she said, aware of the dynamic, hoping, like he, to demystify their roles, to release the tension.

"Helen, I'm not trying to dominate you. But you do have a little-girl-who-wants-approval thing going on, which you're clearly aware of. It's a good example, in fact, of how you twist your receptive essence trait," he said.

"So, it's not very palatable to you, then, I suppose?"

"Well, it is. And it isn't. In one sense it's very sweet because it makes me feel big and strong. It feeds a role I play. But that's why it's also sour . . . because I think it's manipulative and weak. I don't want to feel big and strong because of some obsequious way you're acting; I want to feel big and strong because I am."

"But you *are* big and strong; no one's 'performance' can take that away from you," she said.

"Yes. But I am also small and weak. I see that in my reaction to your reply just now."

"What do you mean?" she asked, feeling excited by a new confession. More anti-seduction. More seduction with language. With trust.

"Well, I was expecting you to get upset at what I just said. My motive in saying that was obviously to stir you—to get you all hot and defensive and angry—feeling small, so I could feel big. I was doing exactly what I don't like: playing a role in order to get you to respond in a particular way so that I could have this feeling about myself . . . and it's a weak, mechanical thing. And I question my motives right now, too. My revealing this to you."

"I think I've met my match," she said.

"For your sake, I hope not," he said.

Her face got red and he said, "I'm sorry. I should be more careful. I meant that—"

"I know, and I appreciate your warning."

"But it wasn't a warning, Helen. . . . Do you want to go for a walk?" he said. "It's a beautiful night."

"Sure, if I can walk. I'm a lightweight; the second cognac did me in," she said, her face flushed from its effects.

"I'll help you. The fresh air will be good, too."

And he took her arm and helped her up. Helen noticed all the eyes on them as they walked alongside the bar toward the door. And it wasn't just that they both were tall and good-looking and wore fine clothes. It was their presence. Ed turned to the bartender, "Peace be with you, my friend."

"And with you, Ed—and Helen," said the bartender.

Ed seemed pleased the bartender knew her—that his eyes twinkled when he said her name.

"Goodnight, Terry," she said, smiling at him as he filled two mugs of beer.

"Careful, Helen, Moses here is known for his magic," Terry said.

"I don't doubt that!" she said, and then tripped on the bottom of a barstool. Ed took her hand and lifted her into the air practically.

"I shouldn't have let you go . . . I won't do it again."

And they walked toward the river, Ed holding her.

## *all things considered*
(*con:* with; *sider:* stars)

Just when you mean to tell her
that you have no gifts to give her,
she gets you on her wave-length
and she lets the river answer
That you've always been her
lover.
      —*Leonard Cohen*

He walked slow. And steady. It was a nice pace, comfortable. She felt her hip spooned into his. For just one moment she realized that she was arm in arm, hip to hip with a man she had only met once before. But in so many ways she *had* met him before. And before and before and before. They walked in the direction of the river.

"As seductive as it all is—the book—I think you got the love stuff all wrong," he said.

"More baiting the hook?" she said.

"No. More truth," he said.

"All right, but it's not about *me* getting it, anyway; it's about the reader getting it. Whatever they get. But what do you mean?"

"What I *mean* is that the *real* epilogue should be one where you learn to love from yourself, because you have an abundance of love already within yourself, because you have made it there; one where you learn to love not because you have been aroused or because you have successfully aroused another."

"I think I wanted the reader to decide for themselves about love," she said.

"But do they come away with the key?"

"I'm not sure. I want them to come away with what they need. What key?"

"The key to love."

"The key to love? Oh, what is it, master guru?" she said.

"All right, my sweet little disciple . . . the key to love is . . . attention. It's being interested even after it's boring, after the mystery is gone. Because *that's* when the real realness makes itself known."

"Oh. Is this a justification for a loveless, boring marriage?"

"No. Something else. My ex-wife used to say—"

"Ex-wife? Sorry to interrupt but, I don't understand. All this great talk and you're divorced?"

"Yeah. She left me . . ."

"Ahw . . . I'm sorry," she said softly.

"For Evan."

"For *Evan?*"

"Yes, Evan."

"Jesus! No *wonder* the story made you sick!"

"Yes, yet another reason," he said, lighting a cigarette.

"When was this?"

"The divorce? Three years ago . . ."

"What happened?"

"Evan, for one. But, I think the problem was, though I loved her, I had never been in love with her . . . and I think I pushed her away. . . . I don't think I've ever really allowed myself to fall in love."

"Well, that seems hard to believe. Maybe it's just a definition problem. Maybe you've been in love but you called it something else."

"I don't know."

"But you loved her, now what do you mean by that . . . what did that feel like?"

"Well, when I worked on it, it felt like . . . like spinning light from darkness in the centrifuge of *watching.*"

"Uhgh, Ed! That sounds just *awful!*"

"It's not. It's good. It's very good. It's love of god. Love of essence. A feeling of oneness. A merging, melting feeling— that preverbal infant-mother thing, before there was a sense of self and other."

"I think I've had glimpses of that. . . ."

"There's a way to get more than glimspes, you know."

"Yes, I know . . . 'the work' . . . But . . . what happened with Evan and your ex-wife? Obviously it didn't last."

"Yes . . . that's right, it didn't last. He met another woman not long after they got together, and left her. She's in Oregon now, raising sheep."

"*Jesus!* Yikes! How can you bear to work with him, to live with him at Solaren? To teach him?"

"It's all a part of 'the work,' Helen. I love him like a brother. He just needs more work on attention. We all do. Humanity has one big Attention Deficit Disorder. . . . But I'm curious about *you.* I have the impression you *have* allowed yourself to fall in love. And I'm a little envious."

"I really don't understand you. Your teachings are really against being in love aren't they?"

"If it's mechanical, yes. If it's really love . . . no."

"Well, you're right, I've been in love. And it's what I tried to explore in *Conscious Shock*. I called it the *hot love/warm love* meme. It's romantic love versus companionate love, I think. Being in hot, romantic love, there is never a chance to think. Never. Not a gulp of air. Nothing. No control. No sense of self. Just 'other.' Just feeling. No thoughts. No *thought* about being *selfless,* just selfless . . .

"But the paradox is, we can look at that and see that it's really selfish, right? To be unthinking is selfish. The mechanicalness of it doesn't really leave room for you to consider the other person, even though that's all it feels like you're doing. And for me, it's a little related to the madonna/whore dichotomy—maternal love versus sexy love.

"I think, companionate, filial, spiritual love . . . the kind you and everyone at Solaren are trying to practice, has a similar paradox, just in reverse. It's like you start from that idea . . . that hot love is selfish and that to really love requires consciousness and work. But, without the feeling of real 'love' (the selfish body kind), 'the work' falls apart. There's no glue. Only one's intention, one's will. And that seems to be a head thing, not a heart thing. You need—"

His cell phone began ringing. He looked at the incoming number.

"I have to take this call, sorry . . ."

"That's okay," she said, amused at him—this seemingly incongruous cell phone-answering, hard liquor-drinking, smoking guru.

"Hello? . . . *Marhaba salam alekom*, Muqad . . . *kowiees* . . . good, good . . . yes, I *myself* will be there. Yes, I look forward to it. Eight-o-five. JFK. Alitalia. Flight six-ten; gate thirty-four. Yes,

yes, customs . . . yes. *Naam. Ahlan wa sahlan. . . . . Inshaalha. Maasalaama."*

"Arabic?" she asked.

"Yes. Muqad's a master teacher of Guerttiev movements. He was calling from the plane. He's coming from Iran to teach at Solaren for a few months. He's a little anxious, though—afraid of rednecks . . . but I told him how liberal Hundton is. But of course we aren't far from redneck country . . . but he's not going to leave Solaren . . . so I'm not worried about him."

She was hooked. The language. The intrigue. The foreignness. The fact that he was going to be driving six hours just one way to pick up this man when there must have been an easier way.

"I've been doing some work with this group FAAR, Fight Against Arab Racism. He's right to be afraid," she said.

"What kind of work?"

"Well, I do a lot of work with progressive groups here, actually. For them, I go to meetings mostly, to work on educating tolerance. And we've done a few protests on campus."

"Yes. Those are nice reconciling forces, but basically useless."

"Useless? Was it useless when I volunteered as a grief counselor for the family and friends of that Muslim gas station attendant who was pummeled to death? Is the money I give to various charities to help victims of racism useless?"

"Well, it's not useless. But it is. The aim is to keep your eye on the bigger picture—to look at the root cause of this."

"I know that. But in the meantime, you have to take action and help."

"Yes. It's okay. But what needs to be done is to transform human consciousness. And we do that, we work toward the evolution of human wisdom, through our own transformation."

"Okay, Ed. But when I was over supporting that gas station attendant, protesting and meeting with his family, you guys at Solaren were planting a garden for him—that's what I read in the paper. A garden! There's got to be a way to reconcile the high ideal with the reality. To do both. Though you know I like the ideal. And I admire your intentions."

"And I admire yours. I think what is useful is that you respond with strength, from yourself, to whatever opportunities your life presents, and that is good."

They stared at each other for a long time. They did admire each other. Admired their differences—and the similarities, too.

"When is it you pick Ma. . . ?"

"Muqad . . . Eight tomorrow morning."

"That's in eight hours. Will you get any sleep?" she asked.

"No. And it's best if I don't. We don't need as much sleep as we think we do. . . . Will you come with me? I'd love your company."

It seemed so loony, the whole thing, and yet she felt pulled by it. She loved feeling pulled. Desire. Desire to be with him. Desire to stay up all night driving to pick up some Guerttievian Arab guy.

"Okay, yes, but do I get to sleep?"

"No . . . you get to talk to me incessantly so I don't fall asleep at the wheel!"

"Ah, I see."

"No. I'm just kidding. You can sleep whenever you like. I just want your company. You smell good."

And they walked back to the bar where Ed's MG was parked.

⁀

Car talk was really different than walk talk, she thought. Not better. Not purer. Just different. Helen used to talk a lot with her dad in the car when she was little, maybe there was something to that. But there was more. The loss of control as the passenger. The feeling of anticipation, of destination. The movement. Time and space. Less grounded, less chthonic, more male.

"I like your idealism. It makes me angry, too," she said, looking ahead.

"It hooks you, doesn't it?" he said.

"You bastard! Yeah, it does a little."

"That's what all your male characters lacked . . . well, except for that Irish mole."

"Yes. It's true . . . it's a terribly good hook for me, on many levels. . . . My father was an idealist. Though he was also very much a materialist. You're really an idealist in both senses of the word, which is especially interesting to me. Anyway, my dad was this . . . this leader of this . . . communist group. And about twenty years ago, he was helping to organize some peasants down in Nicaragua and he was . . . killed—"

"My god, Helen, I'm sorry, that's horrible."

"Yeah, I was away at college at the time. It was . . . my mother is *still* trying to uncover what happened and still goes there every year to interview people and to just be there."

"My goodness. Have you been?"

"Yeah, twice. And I'm not going back . . . but I don't want to talk about it."

"Okay," he said.

And he took a cigarette from near the gearshift.

"Light this for me, will you?" he said, putting the cigarette in his mouth.

He handed her a matchbook.

"Sure," she said, lighting the match and holding it still for him. "It's a pretty box."

"They're Turkish."

"Where's the pipe?"

"I just smoke that when I'm at the farm. I don't know why."

"That's weird."

"Yeah, I guess . . . You were going to tell me about your hook . . . your father . . ."

"That's right. I think a hook for me is a man who wants to try to change the world in some way, though not necessarily 'by any means necessary.' And I think, evolutionarily, there's a hook there, too. It's ambitious. It's a signal of intelligence, status and power, and possibly resources, but also caring . . . all things women, according to EP theory, look for in long-term mates. But I think it's deeper than all of that. I think I'm attracted to it just for its pure goodness. In some ways it can't be analyzed. It's beyond evolutionary theory, Freudian theory, social psychology. It's almost memetic . . . Like the 'desire for the good of humanity' in me, is attracted to the desire for it, in you . . . as if it's built in and perpetuating itself."

"Well, I'm glad to know you're not as analytical and heavily into that EP shit as you sounded in your story," he said.

"I'm into figuring it out. Human nature. Our purpose too. Who we are, why we do what we do. And I'll use any models and maps I can to get as close as I can to an answer. As limiting as it is, EP theory is the best answer we have now. But it'll be replaced at some point, no question.

"As far as how I came across in the manuscript, friends who've read *Conscious Shock* think they're reading about *me*—think they have some insight. . . . And yes, I'm in there some, but also not. It's fiction. There's something higher at work than my ego here. I wrote it without worrying about what people would think about me. I wrote what was needed. In a way, I let it get written rather than write it. In a way the characters are *memes*—not *me*. I think it would have suffered if I worried about my self-picture. Or not gotten written. Perhaps it suffers anyway, but it would have been worse if I thought about how I came across. Whatever it is, it's liberating."

"I think that's wonderful. You're a little crazy-wise."

"Crazy-wise? What's that?"

"It's from Shambhala warrior practice. Crazy wisdom is . . . not caring what others think, nor for the implications or results of what one does and says. A crazy-wise person doesn't try to translate falseness into truthfulness. She leaves it alone. It's about being free."

"Well, I fight with that, of course. I care and don't care what others think. Like last month, there was a bag on my porch from students with a note asking me to donate cans of food to some Native Americans in Arizona. I'm not sure why it was this particular place, it seemed so distant and remote. And I thought, well, that's nice . . . but won't it cost more to get the cans there than it's worth? Wouldn't it be better if I sent money? And so that's what I did. I put my energy into finding out where to send money and sent it. Saw the bag thing as a nice college gesture, but perhaps not terribly useful. But I had to deal with the fact that my neighbors did the bag thing and I didn't. The disapproving looks.

"And you know what? A couple of the kids in my epistemology class were really acting strange and I just got to the bottom of it this week . . . they were the ones who came to collect from my porch . . . and they knew it was my house . . . and they thought I was a real skinflint. The thing is, we live in social communities where we're affected by our external actions. Reputation is important. The EP literature has a lot on that.

"I don't want to worry about what others think. Try not to. Most of the time, *don't*. I'd rather put my energy into something real rather than micromanage my appearance for others. And yet, when I don't worry, it often smacks me down hard! And then I have to worry again. . . . People only know what they see and hear. Maybe it's a balance . . . and I think we all, *all* struggle with this."

"Yes, as far as other's opinions about you . . . it *is* a consideration, particularly if they're ignorant and judgmental and impressionistic. You have to be as careful as you have to be to protect yourself from the results of ignorance, though of course, it doesn't matter what they think of you except to the extent that they'll impede your progress toward your aim."

"It must be nice to have an aim so clearly defined, the way you do over at Solaren. That sounded almost textbook."

"Yes, it's easier to know when you're off the path if you actually have one and if it's clearly marked," he said, taking the last drag of his cigarette and flicking it out the window.

"Hey, Mr. crazy-wise, why not use the ashtray?"

"I'm sorry, you're right," and he looked at her and smiled, like they had been doing this for years.

"Ed? I'm going to close my eyes now."

"Okay, Helen, sweet dreaming."

"Goodnight . . ."

⌒

It was another gorgeous evening in Hundton. The night of their return from the crazy airport day.

Helen and Ed were back at the river sitting on the mushroom log, not even tired. He had wanted her to meet him at Solaren, at the yurt, but she wasn't ready. It had too much of the feeling of repeating something, and anyway, she was afraid to run into Evan. In time she would accept the inevitable understanding of the repetition and resign herself to correcting it. Re-righting it; rewriting it. But not this night. It wasn't time.

"Mmm, do you smell that?" she said, inhaling deeply.

"A sweetness? Yes, I smell it a little, it's wonderful. What is it? Is it you?"

"No . . . black locust blossoms . . . you can't see them yet. . . . they seem to blossom at the top of the trees first; I guess because the sun hits them there first. But you can smell them—almost more than when the blossoms are closer to the ground. Do you know them?"

"No. Only from your story. Someone couldn't smell them and I thought, what's a black locust blossom?"

"Yes, a not-so-lovely name for one of the more heavenly scents I know. It's a wonderful tree. Pioneers used them as posts. They have incredibly long root systems and grow fast. And their blossoms not only smell good, they're beautiful, too . . . they look like white elongated grape clusters. It's not that strong a smell to you, though, is it?"

"No, not that strong. I smoke, maybe that's why. It's really strong to you, though, isn't it?"

"Yeah, it's very strong. . . . Women generally have better noses than men, you know."

"Yes, I have noticed that. What's that about? You must have some theory."

"Well, of course. I can think of all sorts of evolutionary explanations: Since women dealt with gathering food and its preparation, good noses were important, selected for, and survived. Also for smelling children, their health and sickness. You know you can smell sickness? I always know when my children are getting sick from their smell, and there's an advantage to that. I can start to take care of them, strengthen them, before they get sicker."

At first she regretted saying that. It was the truth and what was on her mind, but she feared it sounded like she was *trying* to sound like a good mother. Like she was trying to hook him with it. But she was so sick of editing things because of what they seemed to be doing. She just couldn't worry about whether or not that's what he was thinking. So what if he thought she said that to hook him? What was the sense in not saying the truth or what was on her mind? To edit it would just be a manipulation for some end. (Mother Nature certainly liked this crazy-wise view of just "say whatever"—it was allowing Her to do what *She* wanted to do.)

"And, of course, choosing mates . . . smelling their phero-mones and other emanations, also for clues to signs of their health, their immune systems. Men, on the other hand, are more visual, as you know . . . hunting, tracking, using visual cues to determine health and fecundity in women. But you hate this stuff, don't you?"

"I don't hate it . . . I see it as limiting, horizontal instead of vertical, but I also think it's interesting. And there must be something to it."

"Yes, there's something to it. But enough EP," Helen said smiling. "I want to talk about this 'will' thing, the conscious love thing, it confuses me."

"You're obsessed with love. I think you need to get out of the mind a little."

"Well that sounds great, but this is all I know how to do right now."

"Okay. What is it? What confuses you?"

"Well, it seems the classic romantic notion of love is that there is only *one* key that fits our lock . . . but Guerttiev's seems to be that any key fits . . . that we are all master keys because we *are* love and have love within us, right? But I don't think so. You can't *will* love. There has to be some automatic, mechanical *something* going on. There *has* to be a hook. There has to be some deep link: a physical, chemical, pheromonal, genetic, essential complementarity and attraction. *Something!* But there also has to be some psychological and 'personality' connection, stemming from experience as a child and through-out life. And then there has to be some practical connection:

intellectual, intentional, purposeful . . . It's that trine theory of love I have: evolution, experience, culture . . . the three layers . . . All three have to be working in some form . . . or forget the will! The will won't matter! The will can't matter . . . there won't be will! Maybe what the will does is glue these three together . . . or fills in the gaps so the key fits the lock."

"All you need is *attention*," he said.

"You're not even listening, are you? I think you guys are afraid of that first layer, the deep one, the material, body one. You discount it and yet you are drawn to it. Evan's tortured by it. I think you are, too. You think you have the answer because you've read so damn much about this . . . teach it, but you yourself have never been in love. Something's wrong here. I mean, are we simply talking about conditional versus unconditional love here? Is that what it's about? Yes, beauty fades. Attraction fades. There's always another delicious, young thing popping up on your radar screen. Is that what you're struggling with?"

"Guerttiev said, 'Faith of consciousness is freedom; faith of feeling is weakness and faith of body is stupidity.'"

"That's not an answer . . . Okay . . . I say, screw most of that! Know what I say? Faith of body is *intelligent*, and faith of feeling is *strength*. I find your whole fear of the body and feelings to be primitive and dualistic . . . I mean, you need it all. The subterranean and the heavenly. The body and mind. Our animalness and Godliness. Instinct and Will . . . To deny one is to deny our humanness. It's a fear . . . it really is a contraction. I don't think you can truly love without it all. To really love is to accept that mechanicalness . . . it can't truly be transcended . . . or then we're not human. I think the most brave thing is not to turn against one or the other. Science, the body. Religion, the soul . . . I think the way toward real freedom is in the reconciliation. The union. *Religscien* . . . to tie together knowledge . . . or something like that."

"You're your favorite guru, aren't you?"

"I never said I was a guru, Ed. I think you hold that lofty distinction."

"I think that was your word. I'm a teacher. Founder of Solaren. I have genuine knowledge on how to develop, and so I guide those who seek a psychotransformative way. And I do it within a community because that is the only way to do 'the work.'"

"I think you're all full of shit. I say, walk the talk, Mr. Ed!"

"Hey, watch it, Ms. Mercurial . . . And don't you mean horse shit, then?"

"Oh, you're very clever. I guess you have an off the charts genius IQ just like Evan, *huh?*"

"I do. Doesn't mean anything . . . you know that."

"Of course . . ."

"Did you love Evan?" Ed said, twirling a small tree branch.

And she sat there thinking a while, watching him. Almost computing.

"No, I don't think I did," she said, finally. "I wanted to. I had love feelings sometimes. Maybe if I had trusted him . . . Maybe if . . . I don't know. I think I've been loved out for the longest time. . . . I really don't think I can love anyone."

"Here we go! Helen. That's ridiculous. You just need . . . need . . . *shock* treatment, an—"

"Look who's talking . . ."

"Hey, I'm the guru here and don't interrupt me," he said, giving her a wink.

"I'm sorry, go ahead."

"You have to stop thinking you've experienced everything, Helen. . . . It keeps you in a cocoon of inertia. You don't know anything. Neither do I, not even what I just said! *Summa sciencia nihil scire*—Socrates. It means—"

"I know: 'The height of science is to know nothing.'"

"That's right . . . Well, you know what Guerttiev says?"

"What?"

"'Patience is the mother of will. Without will, how can you be born?'"

"Be patient? For love? Why? Should the Sahara be patient for water? Should the ape be patient for language? Patience isn't what I need. Just acceptance of my fate. This is who I am now, what I've become. This is it."

"Helen, you've got to be joking! I mean, talk about *awful*, woman! You might as well just end it all!"

"What? This is it. I'm this way for a reason. There's really no turning back. I've seen the truth. Or maybe it's just that I'm callused and protected for a reason. Maybe there'll be a day when the calluses wear off and I feel again. And that will be nice. But I can't will it."

"But you can work at it. You can work on those calluses. . . . Look, you sound stuck. And I'm stuck, in my own way . . . But I think the only thing worth striving for is to become *un*stuck."

"I guess . . . but I don't place any particular value on my not falling in love. I don't see it as the goal. It just is what it is. And if I'm meant to fall in love again, and *do*, well, I'll place no value on that either."

"But Helen, that *is* the goal. Love is the goal."

"Oh," she said. "I didn't know."

He smiled at her. He liked her humor, her presence, her sometimes subtlety.

"You know," he said, "I had a thought about your story."

"Yeah, what kind of thought?"

"For a different ending."

"A different ending? That's funny . . . what is it?"

"Well, if the woman in 'Siren's Song' —what was her name?"

"She didn't have a name."

"Right. That's right. Well . . . so you have your nameless protagonist tell Caleb that she miscarried, but then actually have Caleb's baby."

"Hmm, that would make it interesting . . ."

"Yes, then you can have her lie to her husband that it's *his*—like those zebra finches she writes about. I think it would wrap the triptych up quite nicely."

"You're a good reader. You really thought about this. . . . But I'm not so sure about that. I'm not exactly sure what it does for the story. First of all, lying to her husband pretty much goes against her character and nature. . . ."

"Well, that in itself would be interesting. . . ."

"I guess . . . but I'm not interested in that, in changing her character. But I suppose she *could* have the baby and tell her husband the *truth*—that it's Caleb's . . ."

"No, Helen. No. Let that be her secret and hers alone. Let it be the point of suffering, the sacrifice that is like the thorn digging deeper that reminds her that her aim and duty is to love—like God's relegation of Lucifer to the netherworld, as a kind of reminding factor, a secret polarization of the universe. . . . She is being true to the possible realization of the Truth. Something like your Indian child in 'Red Love' who was given to the white family."

"No, *Ed!* No! The ending should be about her art . . . that *that* is what she has created and what is significant. To end with her having Caleb's baby and duping her husband into raising the child as if it were his, negates the importance of her development—of her integrating the masculine side of herself—of her loving and accepting that side of herself—of her creating art. Maybe it's because you're a man, but I don't like your ending . . . I want her to be strong. . . . Having Caleb's baby and lying to her husband that it is *his*—doesn't seem like a very strong or smart, or emancipated move," she said.

"Ah, but Helen, art can't save her, only love can," he said.

"Yes," she said, "but if there's one thing I'm beginning to learn finally, it's that there *is* no love without art."

And they fell in love under the stars.

And they felt love the next night, and the night after that, and the night when they made the sweetest love of her life on the pillows in the yurt.

But that's another story.